Toby's Story

A Dog's Purpose Puppy Tale

Also by
W. Bruce Cameron

Toby's Story

A Dog's Purpose Puppy Tale

W. Bruce Cameron

Illustrations by
Richard Cowdrey

STARSCAPE

A Tom Doherty Associates Book
New York

TOBY'S STORY

Copyright © 2019 by W. Bruce Cameron

Reading and Activity Guide copyright © 2019 by Tor Books

Illustrations © 2019 by Richard Cowdrey

A Starscape Book
Published by Tom Doherty Associates
175 Fifth Avenue
New York, NY 10010

www.tor-forge.com

Library of Congress Cataloging-in-Publication Data

Names: Cameron, W. Bruce, author. | Cowdrey, Richard, illustrator.
Title: Toby's story / W. Bruce Cameron ; illustrations by Richard Cowdrey.
Description: First edition. | New York, NY : Tom Doherty Associates, 2019. |
    Series: A dog's purpose puppy tale | "A Starscape Book." | Summary: Toby,
    an unusually calm beagle puppy, finds his purpose when Mona and her mother
    adopt him and teach him to be a therapy dog at a nursing home.
Identifiers: LCCN 2018056055| ISBN 9780765394989 (hardcover : alk. paper) |
    ISBN 9780765395009 (ebook)
Subjects: LCSH: Beagle (Dog breed)—Juvenile fiction. | CYAC: Beagle (Dog
    breed)—Fiction. | Dogs—Fiction. | Animals—Infancy—Fiction. | Working
    dogs—Fiction. | Humananimal relationships—Fiction.
Classification: LCC PZ10.3.C1466 To 2019 | DDC [Fic]—dc23
LC record available at https://lccn.loc.gov/2018056055

Our books may be purchased in bulk for promotional, educational, or business use.
Please contact your local bookseller or the Macmillan Corporate and Premium
Sales Department at 1-800-221-7945, extension 5442, or by email
at MacmillanSpecialMarkets@macmillan.com.

First Edition: May 2019

Printed in the United States of America

0 9 8 7 6 5 4 3 2 1

For Ellery, Rhedyn, and Shelby

Toby's Story

A Dog's Purpose Puppy Tale

1

The first smells were exactly what I expected, even if I didn't know *why* I expected them: Warm fur. Sweet milk. That was my mother, who smelled like safety and food and love. I could also sense my brothers and sisters, who smelled—well, a lot like me.

We all huddled close together. There was comfort in the closeness and in the heat of furry bodies. Even if a brother was sleeping on my head or a sister was sucking on my ear, I didn't mind. We were together. That was all that mattered.

But even then, there was another smell. Sometimes I would lift my head as far up as my weak little neck could get it, and twitch my nose, and there it would be.

It was a smell of fresh, moving air. It was a smell of green things that were full of life. It was a smell that made me want to know more about it.

But I had to get bigger and stronger before I was ready to find out what this other smell might be.

In a few days, my eyes blinked open for the first time. I saw a great big head with soft brown fur and a white blaze down the nose. Dark eyes looked at me fondly, and a wet tongue came out and licked me all over, from nose to tail, in a few swipes. That was my mother.

I loved her. She was wonderful!

When I looked away from my mother, I saw puppies all around me. Their fur was brown and black in splotches. My mother licked them, too, and we all wiggled forward to get a turn at her delicious milk.

Then we fell asleep. Being awake was hard work.

I liked it, though. Each time my eyes opened, I was able to stay awake longer. I was able to see more of what surrounded me. My family and I lived in a dark box with an open door. Through that door I could sometimes see glimpses of bright sky. And I could smell that exciting smell, the one that made my nose twitch each time it wafted my way.

Now and then a man came to the door. He would squat down and talk gently to my mother, and sometimes she got up and walked away from my brothers and sisters and me to greet him and wag her tail.

"Good girl, Sadie," the man would say to my mother, rubbing her head. "You're such a good mom."

That was how I found out that my mother's name was Sadie.

At first, all of us pups would peep and squeal forlornly for our mother to come back, but before long, we could get up on our feet and stagger over to greet the man as well.

I had thought that my mother was huge, but this man was gigantic! His hands were as big as my whole body, and they smelled amazing. I could not stop sniffing and licking them. I picked up smells of other animals, and something deep and rich and mysterious, and more of that fabulous fresh odor that I loved so much.

Where did all these smells come from? From outside the door, I was sure. I was determined to find out.

As soon as my legs were strong enough, I lurched out the door. Both of my brothers and all three of my sisters piled out after me. Two sisters bumped into my tail and tipped me forward onto my nose.

That's when I found out that the mysterious smell on the man's hands had been dirt—the stuff that was now all over my face. It was superb! I loved it! I sniffed hard, licked my mouth, and realized that dirt does not taste as good as it smells.

Oh well. I wobbled back up and looked around.

Later I learned that the place I was seeing for the

first time was called the Ranch. To me, at that moment, it was outside. Outside was big. And very interesting. I turned my head this way and that, taking in the sights and sounds and smells all around me.

We were in a space closed in on all sides by fences made of wire. Inside our space was dirt and grass and bowls with water. One of my sisters had already fallen into one of the bowls. Inside the space, also, was the little shed where my brothers and sisters and I had been born.

Outside of the wire, I could see more dirt and more grass. Far away was another pen with very big, long-legged dogs inside it. One of them actually had a person riding on its back. Astonishing!

Through the wire also came that scent that I had always longed to know more about. It was the scent of fresh air moving fast enough to ruffle my fur and make my ears sway. It carried other odors along with it—the green, living smell I had already noticed, along with the smells of other animals, fur, breath, sweat, dung, and urine. But there was something about the air, that sweet, warm air, that made me want to run.

So I did. I raced around the pen as fast as my short legs could take me. As soon as my brothers and sisters saw me running, they yipped with excitement and chased after me, dashing forward, stumbling, falling down, getting back up. Our tongues hung out, and our tails wagged madly. Pretty soon, there was no way to tell if they were chasing me or if I was chasing them, but it was all so marvelous I didn't care.

Running! I loved running! It was wonderful!

In time, we were so exhausted that we all had to fall in a heap and take a nap. But after that, we all burst out of our house every chance we got and ran as much as we could.

The man came to see us often in the pen. I found out that his name was Walt, and after a while, I realized that he lived in a very large shed of his own—a house, people call it—nearby. He would come out of that building every morning and head right for us. He had a power that astounded me—he could cause a section of the fence to swing wide open, letting him walk right into our pen. No matter how hard I tried, I never could figure out a way to do that myself.

Walt would step through the fence, sit on the ground, and talk to my mother, Sadie. She'd lick his face and sniff his clothes before hurrying back to check on us.

Walt would stay sitting on the ground, and my brothers and sisters and I always raced over to him. We piled into his lap and gnawed on his shirt and licked his fingers while he laughed.

Once, his hands caught me and held me belly-up for

a few moments, while I wiggled indignantly. It was not comfortable, plus I couldn't snuggle into his shirt while he held me like that.

Walt chuckled and turned me back over. He held me up close to his face. I licked his nose and his chin and as much of his cheek as I could reach.

"Okay, boy," he said with a chuckle. "Toby. I think you're going to be Toby."

He set me down on the dirt again, but I clambered back up onto his lap while he picked up one of my sisters the same way he'd picked me up. I wasn't fooled, though. I knew I was his favorite.

"Tabitha," he said, putting my sister down. I seized hold of his shirt between my teeth and wrestled with it while he picked up more puppies. My other two sisters were named Tamara and Tess. My brothers became Titus and Timothy.

It didn't matter what we were called. What mattered was that we were together and that we could run every day, smelling the remarkable fresh fragrance that made my tail wag so madly it just about knocked me over into the dirt.

I loved that smell so much that after Walt left, I pressed my nose into a corner of our pen and stood there, sniffing as hard as I could. The fence sagged a little under my weight, and that's when I noticed a gap between a post and the wire attached to it.

I pushed my nose into that gap. It opened a little wider.

My whole head followed my nose. I shoved with my back legs and scrabbled with my front claws. And then I was through! I was outside the fence! I was doing Walt's trick!

My brothers and sisters—Tabitha, Tamara, Tess, Titus, and Timothy—came racing over to see what had happened to me. It only took them a few moments to wiggle through the fence as well. Our mother came to the gap and put her nose through, but she was too big to fit. She barked impatiently, warning us to come back.

But we couldn't return to the pen. There was so much running to be done!

I dashed this way and that across thick grass that was tall enough to tickle my belly. Dandelions batted my head, and a long, skinny bug with powerful legs sprang up right in front of my nose. I stopped and sat down hard, and Tess crashed into me. I barked at the bug as it whirred away into the grass.

I chased it and Tess chased me. Chasing things was the best!

I couldn't find the bug again, but it didn't matter that much, because I was suddenly brought up against another pen with a wire fence like ours. There were no puppies inside this fence, however. Something different was in there—feathery animals that each had two scratchy, scaly feet.

They were jerky, pecky birds that I would one day learn were called chickens.

I barked at them to tell them I was Toby. To tell them they could come out and play and run with us. But the chickens didn't seem to get the message. One of them shook out her wings and stretched out her neck and suddenly rushed at the fence—right at me!

I yelped. She was bigger than I was! And she had a very sharp beak that pecked at my toes through the wires.

I ran away. That chicken did not know how to play! But she was in a pen and I was out, so it didn't matter. Nothing mattered but tearing across the soft grass with my brothers and sisters.

That delicious smell poured into my nose as I ran. It was the smell of the whole world when I was running as fast as I could, the most wonderful thing in a place full of wonders.

I was so busy with this smell that I didn't even notice another scent creeping up on me as I ran. So I almost thumped right into a strange animal crouched in the grass. It was female; I could smell that. It had wide yellow eyes that stared at me, and it narrowed them as I got close.

It looked . . . interesting.

My brother Timothy was right behind me, and he liked this new animal, too. I think he noticed, just as I did, the way her back legs were bunched underneath her, and the way the muscles all along her back were tight. She was ready to jump. To spring away.

That meant we could chase her!

I slowed down. Step by step, I went closer to this new animal. Timothy was right beside me. Any moment now, she was going to run away. I just knew it. Another step closer . . . another . . .

The animal had triangular ears that stood up straight on her head. But when I took another step, she put those ears back flat against her skull and opened her mouth. I thought she was about to bark, but instead she let out a strange, threatening hiss. Her tiny teeth looked sharp!

It was such a confusing sound, I stopped, trying to figure out what she meant. Timothy didn't stop, though. He kept going. Another step . . . another . . .

The animal's fur fluffed up on her back, making her look suddenly bigger. I began to think that Timothy might not have the right idea here.

Suddenly, the animal let out a screech that hurt my ears. Then she did something truly surprising.

She didn't run away! She didn't let us chase her. Instead, she shot out a paw and batted Timothy hard on the nose.

He was so surprised, he fell over. I hurried to his

side and sat on him. It just seemed like the right thing to do. He wiggled out from under me and chewed on my leg, and when we both looked up, the animal was calmly licking the paw she had used to swat Timothy.

She clearly had no idea how to play. We decided to punish her by ignoring her. I chased Timothy back toward the chickens, and he turned around and chased me back toward the pen. Walt was waiting there, and he scooped me up in his big hands.

"Escape artist, huh?" he asked me, and he plopped me back inside the pen. Timothy trotted in a few seconds later. My other littermates were already there, curled up with our mother for some dinner. "And I guess you learned to leave the cat alone."

I barreled over to join my family. I loved my mother's milk as much as I loved running through the grass with that wind smell in my nose. I loved discovering the chickens and the other animals. I loved falling asleep in a warm pile with a brother on either side of me and a sister's head in the middle of my back.

I loved everything.

Except the cat.

2

 The next morning, I hurried over to examine that gap in the fence, ready to get out and run in the grass and maybe visit the chickens again or ignore that cat. But to my surprise, no matter how hard I pushed my nose against the wire, it would not budge. The gap was gone, and Walt's scent was painted all over the place.

I had to be content with chasing Titus and Tabitha around our pen. That was fun, but not as much fun as running outside, where there was more room and more to smell. When would I get outside again?

About that time, our mother began to grow restless when we'd snuggle up to her and feed. Once or twice, she even got up and moved away from us, leaving us yipping for more.

On one of those days, Walt came into the pen with a bowl in each hand. Something in those bowls smelled exciting. It made my tail wag eagerly.

When Walt set the bowls down, I dashed over to investigate one of them. Inside was a soft brown mush. I stuck my nose into it and sniffed hard. Then I had to sneeze and shake my head to get brown blobs off my muzzle.

Titus licked my face to help get it clean. My other brother and sisters were sniffing and licking the stuff in the bowl. I saw Tess bite at it. That seemed like a good idea, so I shook Titus off, stuck my nose back into the bowl, and took a bite.

It was awesome!

Eating rather than drinking was a little strange at first, but the mush tasted so good, I didn't want to stop. When the bowl was empty, there was mush on my nose and feet and fur and on the grass beneath my paws, but there was some in my belly as well.

The next day, Walt brought more of the mush, and we all knew what to do right away. And once the bowls were empty, he did something even more exciting.

He opened the gate to our pen!

We dashed outside, bumping into each other in our

eagerness to explore. Something was waiting for us in the grass. A black, square-ish sort of something with four wheels. It was not much bigger than we were, but it was definitely not a puppy.

Later I learned that this kind of thing was called a car. Some cars are much bigger than others (just like some dogs are tiny and some are huge). This was one of the small ones. I approached it and sniffed it thoroughly. It had a very strange smell, one I didn't recognize. It was not dirt, or grass, or water, or fur, or anything that I'd met before.

"Ready to chase the car?" Walt called. I glanced at him. He was standing holding a little shiny black box with both hands. What did he want us to do? I would eat again if that was what he was saying.

Then, to my astonishment, the car moved.

I was shocked. I was pretty sure it was not alive. It had no animal smell to it at all. So how could it move like that?

It lunged forward and then stopped. It did the same thing again. Then it seemed to decide what it wanted, and it zoomed ahead, bumping over the grass.

I barked at it. So did my littermates. Then, suddenly, I knew what I was supposed to do next.

This thing, whatever it was, was running away. I had to chase it. That's what you do to things that run—you chase them!

All of my brothers and sisters had the same idea. Barking and yipping, we raced over the grass after the car. Walt stood nearby. He seemed to be interested in the car, too, because he kept pointing the black box at it.

But Walt didn't chase the car, for some reason. That was my first hint that people don't always understand how to have fun. They need dogs to show them.

I hoped the cat was watching so she would know what to do next time.

The little car might not have been alive, but it was still very clever. It zipped and zoomed this way and that, turning sharply left or right just when one dog or another was about to catch it. Even our mother came out of the pen and joined in the chase. How perfect! How amazing! There was wind in my face, bringing that remarkable smell to me, and all my family was here, and we were chasing something that was running.

There was only one problem. My feet had started to itch. And itch. And itch!

I had to stop running to shake them. Then I dashed forward again. For a few steps, the cool grass felt good against my pads, but then the itching started up again, worse than ever.

I had to sit down and nibble at one of my front feet. Then I had to flop down on my side so that I could get a back foot in my mouth and chew on it. The chewing helped the itching, but as soon as I stopped, it started up again.

I saw that the car had stopped moving. Tamara and Timothy barked at it while Tess climbed on it and fell off. I would have liked to join them, but I was busy at the moment.

Walt came over to sit down next to me.

"Something wrong with your feet, little guy?" he asked me. "Did you get something stuck to them?"

He picked me up and held me upside down so that he could look at all of my feet. I didn't like being held this way, but I did like Walt, so I didn't try to wiggle free.

"Hmmm," he said. "I don't see anything." And he put me back down on the grass.

The car had clearly not finished playing, because it started moving jerkily forward again. I went back to chasing it, but it was not as much fun as before, because I had to keep stopping to gnaw at my feet, trying to get that itch to go away.

That night, I lay with my mother and brothers and sisters, all warm and comfortable together. But I couldn't sleep, not for long. My feet itched so much that they burned, and I kept squirming and waking up and even whimpering a little.

I couldn't understand how my brothers and sisters slept so soundly. Didn't their feet itch, too?

Walt would often let us out of the pen after that. Titus and Timothy and Tess and Tamara and Tabitha were always happy to run over the soft grass and bark at the chickens and sometimes try to teach that car who was boss. (It never learned.)

I wanted to run with them. I wanted to be the one to teach that car its manners or bite a falling leaf or chase down a butterfly. But I didn't always feel like it. My feet never stopped itching. Sometimes I could ignore it, but other times I couldn't, and I would have to lie down and chew on them to try to make things better.

One day when I was lying in our pen, nibbling at one of my front paws, some new people arrived. A man and a boy got out of a big car (not one of the kind that are good to chase) and walked over to us.

Walt was with them, and he opened up the gate and let my brothers and sisters out into the yard. The car was there, waiting for them, and it zoomed ahead while they barked with excitement and tore after it, tails waving.

I did not feel like chasing the car. I had not gotten much sleep the night before, since I had to keep waking up to chew on my feet. I was too tired to chase. I almost felt too tired to be happy.

My mother came over and nudged me with her nose. I could smell and feel her concern, and I licked her cheek. But it did not make my feet feel any better.

"What's wrong with that one?" I heard the boy say.

"I don't know," Walt said, and he sounded puzzled. "He's not sick, as far as I can tell. He just doesn't seem all that lively."

The man and the boy watched all my brothers and sisters chase the car. Tabitha stopped chasing and ran over to the boy to seize one of his shoelaces and wrestle with it fiercely. The boy sat down in the grass, laughing, and Tabitha jumped up to lick his face.

"This one!" the boy said to his father.

"Think she'll make a good hunting dog?" the father asked.

Walt chuckled. "Never seen a beagle yet that wasn't," he answered. "They all love to chase down anything that moves. It's bred into them."

The man and Walt talked a little more, and then the boy scooped up Tabitha in his arms and held her snugly as they walked back toward their car.

I lifted my head and watched them go. My mother barked once and then sat down next to me.

Tabitha was going with this boy, I realized. She would not be coming back.

My sister had been part of my family, but at that moment, I understood that things had changed. She belonged to a new family now. It was a little sad, but it was right, too. Dogs belonged with human families. Human families needed dogs.

I couldn't help wondering whether this new family would have wanted me if I'd chased the car like Tabitha.

The same thing happened again and again in the next few days. People drove up in big cars and watched as my brothers and sisters chased the little car through the grass. Sometimes I would leave the pen with them, but I didn't have the energy to chase the car. It felt better to lie in the shade and nibble at my feet when the itching got too bad.

The new visitors talked with Walt. Lots of them mentioned hunting. "Birds," they'd say. "I need a good bird dog." Or "Got to have one who can go after rabbits."

Often, they'd pick up a puppy and leave.

After a man and a woman had left with Tess, Walt came to sit next to me with a sigh.

"I don't know what I'm going to do with you, Toby," he said, rubbing behind my ears. "You're a cute little guy for sure, but nobody around here is going to pay for a beagle who doesn't want to hunt."

Titus was next to go. Then Timothy left with a family

who had two little girls, and finally Tamara vanished in the arms of a tall, gangly teenage boy.

Walt waved good-bye to the boy who'd taken Tamara and then came and put me back in my pen with my mother.

"Toby boy," he said, and I could hear sadness in his voice. "I can't even give you away for free. I'd hate to take you to a shelter, but this is a working ranch, you know. Everyone here has a job. I can't afford to keep an animal who doesn't do something useful."

I knew he was sad, and I wished I could do something about it. I licked at his hands and then lay down in a patch of dirt with a sigh. I was tired.

My mother came and nudged me with her nose. She walked a few steps away and looked back at me.

I thought she wanted me to do something. What was it?

She came back to nudge me again. This time she ran away. Once again, she stopped and looked back.

I knew what she wanted now. Every dog knows the signal for Chase Me! Was she trying to tell me that if I would only run, I could belong to a family, too?

But I was too busy to run just then. One of my back feet itched and burned. I needed to lick it and bite it, as if the itch were an enemy I could drive away if I were fierce enough. I couldn't chase my mother.

After a few moments, my mother returned to my side. She lay down next to me, curling her body around mine. It felt good, and I leaned into her. She licked the top of my head.

I loved being with my mother. I loved her closeness and her smell and her warmth. But I knew, deep down, that I should belong to a human family, just like my brothers and sisters.

What if I never found my human family? What if nobody wanted me?

3

 It was a few days after that that I heard a car door slam. I was dozing in the shade of the small house where only my mother Sadie and I lived now, and I looked up to see Walt walking toward our pen with a tall woman and a girl beside him.

"I saw your sign out front that said 'Dog Free to a Good Home,'" the woman was saying to Walt. "But . . . oh dear. A beagle?"

"He's so cute!" the girl cried. "Oh, look at him!"

I looked at her. She had dark brown hair that curled around her face and freckles scattered across her nose and cheeks. I wondered how they'd taste.

"He's adorable, Mona," the woman said. "But a beagle's not the right breed for us, I'm afraid. They have so much energy! They need to run all day. That's not going to work."

"Oh . . . ," the girl said sadly. She was staring at me through the wire of the pen.

I stared back at her. I swished my tail back and forth hopefully. Was this my family, come to get me at last?

"Well, Toby's not your usual beagle," Walt said. "Sweet little guy, very friendly, but he doesn't seem to want to run or chase much of anything, so I can't sell him off as a hunting dog like I did his brothers and sisters. I'd hate to have him put down—"

The girl, Mona, gasped.

"—but I don't have room on this place for a dog that just wants to lie around," Walt finished up.

"A dog that wants to lie around is just what we need!" the woman said.

Mona's dark, wide eyes seemed to get even wider. "Really, Mom?"

Walt looked hopeful. "It doesn't bother you that he's a beagle who doesn't run?"

"Well, it's hard to explain," Mona's mother answered. "But I do believe he's going to be perfect. We'll take Toby!"

And that is how I left Walt and the Ranch and my mother and found myself riding along in the back seat of a car, held close in Mona's arms. She felt warm and smelled excellent—sweat from her skin, something

delightfully salty and sweet on her breath, berries in her curly hair. I squirmed so I could get my nose into every wrinkle of her shirt and every crease of her neck. I licked her freckles (which did not taste like much after all) and her mouth.

She laughed. "Mom, he's so friendly! He's going to be perfect!"

"Let's hope so," her mother answered from the front seat.

The car had glass windows, and when I was done smelling and tasting Mona, I wiggled over to put my paws up on one of them and see what was outside. Everything was moving! Trees and bushes and other cars went past in a bewildering blur. I had no idea the world moved so quickly!

Then the car stopped, and the world stopped with it. Holding me snugly, Mona wiggled out of the car. We were outside a very large building. I was used to seeing Walt come in and out of his house, but this building was much bigger.

When we went inside, I discovered something remarkable. The building was full of people!

Did all buildings have this many people? There was a sort of table in front of us, with a woman sitting behind it. She was laughing in an astonished way as Mona put me down on the floor.

The cool tiles felt good on my itchy feet. I was

tempted to lie down and give the pads of my paws a good chewing, but there was so much to see and do! For now, I ignored the itching and kept moving.

A long hallway ran off in one direction, and another in the opposite one. There were doors along each hallway—and people, too. So many people!

Some of the people were sitting in chairs that had big wheels on them. Some were walking slowly, leaning on long sticks. Others seemed to be hurrying as if they had important things to do.

I ran along the hallway, sniffing each new friend eagerly, with Mona right behind me. They smelled . . . interesting. Not like Walt. Walt had smelled of mud and sweat and food and other animals. Most of these people smelled of something unusual, something I had never smelled before. I could not decide if I liked it or not. It was not a smell of the outside world that I was used to. Really, all that it smelled of was clean.

Who would want to be clean when dirty smells were so much more interesting?

A few of the doors were open, and when I peeked inside, I saw beds with *more* people! It was all so overwhelming that I ignored the signals coming from my bladder until they got so powerful that I had to squat right where I was.

"Toby! Not here!" Mona gasped.

She snatched me up before I even got started and

rushed me down the hallway and out through a different door from the one we had come in. We were in a yard with concrete sidewalks and a smooth lawn. At the far side of the lawn was a tall wooden fence with a few trees and bushes growing next to it.

Mona put me down in the grass so I could finish what I'd been doing.

Once I was done, she scooped me up again and cuddled me while I licked at her chin. "You're going to be a great therapy dog, Toby. I just know you will," she told me.

I didn't know what her words meant, but I liked the tone of her voice. I could hear love and approval in it. I loved her, too. I was pretty sure that Mona, and maybe her mother, had just become my human family.

"Listen now, Toby," Mona said, and she sat down on the grass with me in her lap. Her voice sounded serious, and I was a little tired after all the excitement. I plopped down on her legs and nibbled at her fingers just a little so she would know that I liked her as much as she liked me.

"The people here, they need a dog like you. They're old, Toby." She dropped her voice a little, and I could tell she was talking just to me. "Too old to live by themselves anymore, so they come here. And my mom helps take care of them. She's a therapist. There are other people who work here, of course. All the nurses and orderlies, and there's Fran; she's the boss. But, see, people can't do everything. People can give the patients their medicine and help them get into wheelchairs and stuff like that. But they can't really make them happy. That's what you can do, Toby. You can make people happy. And I'll help you, okay? We'll be a team. You and me."

I liked Mona very much. She tasted delicious, and she was very good at scratching along my spine and behind my ears. On my second day in my new home, she brought me a collar with a tag on it that rang like a bell when I shook myself and jangled when I ran.

And the best thing about Mona was this: she talked to me all the time. I didn't understand her words, but I was delighted by her tone of voice. It told me that she loved me and trusted me and that she thought I was important. Out of all the people in my new home, she was my favorite.

But I liked all the people, and I met more and more of them as the days went by. There were the people in the chairs and the people in beds. I visited them regularly. Some fed me treats, which was excellent. Some petted me and talked to me, calling me by my name. "Toby, come," they'd said. "Here, Toby." "Where's Toby?" "Good dog, Toby."

I liked hearing my name over and over, in so many voices. I liked having so many people to greet each day. When I was tired or my feet needed a good chewing,

I'd lie down beside a chair or a bed, and sometimes Mona or her mother would pick me up and put me on a lap or on a soft blanket next to someone who was lying down. I'd take a snooze there, only waking up if my feet itched so badly that I could not stay asleep.

Since I was tired a lot, it was good that my new house had so many laps and so many beds.

"Good dog, Toby," Mona's mother said one day, stroking me as I lay on a bed next to a woman with white hair and very soft skin that gave off a smell of flowers.

Another woman had come into the room and stood there with folded arms. She had gray hair, cut short, and was short and thin herself, with a frown on her face.

"I was skeptical about this whole therapy dog idea, Patsy," she said. I was starting to understand that Mona's mother had two names: Mom to Mona, and Patsy to everybody else. It was confusing, but people are like that. They hardly ever do things the simplest way.

"But I have to admit, you've got me half-convinced," the other woman went on. "That thing isn't half as much trouble as I thought it would be."

"He's perfect, Fran," Mona agreed, rubbing my ears. "He just wants to lie around—and that's what we need him for! I think we can start some real training very soon."

The second woman, Fran, stood watching me for a

little while longer. She stood the way another dog does when he wants someone to know he's in charge—very straight, as tall as she could. Her voice sounded in charge, too. She talked quickly and firmly and a bit louder than Patsy. I understood that she was the boss, and I lowered my head a little and wagged my tail at her to show her that I would not try to question her leadership.

When the white-haired woman began very quietly snoring, Mona came and took me outside to the lawn. After I'd left a puddle soaking into the dirt, I flopped over to gnaw at one of my back paws, which was itching fiercely.

Someone inside pushed the door open. A tall boy came out. I could tell he was young, not a man yet. Puppies don't look or smell like grown-up dogs, and young humans are the same.

The boy had brown hair, lighter than Mona's, that flopped into his eyes, which were squinting a bit in the bright sunlight.

"Hey, a puppy!" he said, and I could hear the pleasure in his voice. He came to kneel beside us. "Can I pet him?"

"Sure," Mona said. "That's his job, being petted! Want to hold him?" She scooped me up and dumped me in the boy's lap.

My foot was still itching and I was ready for a nap,

but I knew I should greet this new person. I got my feet on his chest and licked at his face, tasting something salty and delicious on his mouth that he must have eaten for breakfast. He laughed and used both hands to scratch my back and rub my ears. Once I was done tasting him, I lay down in his lap and closed my eyes.

Mona and the new boy talked a little while his hands stroked my back.

"So . . . are you visiting somebody?" I heard Mona ask.

"Yeah, my grandfather. He's moving in," the boy said. "What about you? Do your grandparents live here or something?"

"No, my mom. I mean, my mom doesn't live here. She works here. She's a therapist. And I come on the weekends a lot. I help out with Toby."

"That's this little guy's name? Toby?"

I thumped my tail sleepily when I heard my name.

"It starts with a *T,* just like mine. I'm Tyler."

"I'm Mona," Mona said. I wagged a bit for her name, too. There was a moment where neither of them talked, although it felt like both of them wanted to.

"So, um, Toby sure seems calm for a beagle," the boy said at last.

"Yeah, he is." Mona sounded relieved to have something to say. "That's why we got him. He's going to be a therapy dog."

"Cool," the boy said. "And you're training him? You must be really good at it. I mean, they don't let kids train dogs usually, I guess."

Mona laughed. I wagged again. "Oh, no, I'm not a real trainer or anything. I've just read some books and stuff, and I like dogs. I want to do that when I grow up, though. Train dogs. I love dogs."

"Me, too. Wish I had one at home. My mom says maybe someday. But I guess it's better not to have one right now. We're going to be coming up here on weekends a lot, visiting my grandfather, making sure he's settled in okay."

"That's good." Mona reached a hand out to pet me, too. I sighed. "Some of the people here, they don't get a lot of visitors. It's really sad for them. Toby's going to help with that. Dogs are great company."

"Yeah, for sure. Hey, can I take Toby to meet my grandfather?"

"Sure you can. He loves new people."

"Um." The boy seemed to hesitate. "Maybe you could come, too?"

Even half-asleep as I was, I felt a funny sort of heat come over Mona, and she seemed not sure what to say. But when I half opened one eye to peek at her, she was smiling. "Yeah. Okay. Sure," she answered. "You carry Toby."

4

 The boy stood up, still holding me, and carried me securely in his arms as he and Mona went inside. I dozed while he took me down the hallway, around a corner, and into a new room.

"Hi, Grandad," he said. "Look, they've got a dog here!" And he put me down on a bed.

I was still sleepy, but I perked up to meet yet another new person. This one was an old man, sitting on the edge of the bed in a room with boxes on the floors and a suitcase open on a chair.

"Well, hello there," the new person said as I crawled onto his lap, the better to sniff at his soft shirt and worn, wrinkled hands. He smelled of tobacco and soap, and he was chewing on something minty. I licked his chin, which was covered with gray whiskers. I'd not yet met a person with fur on his face, just like I had!

"He's Toby," said Mona, who was standing by the door, holding her hands together in front of her and shifting her weight from foot to foot.

"That's Mona," the boy said. "She's training Toby. He's going to be a therapy dog."

"Glad to hear it," the old man said. "Nothing like a dog to make a place feel like home." His voice was low and raspy, but kind. "A person who trains dogs has to have a good heart," he said, looking keenly at Mona. "Tyler doesn't have a girlfriend, you know. Do you have a boyfriend?"

Mona got even hotter than she had outside, and her face turned a different shade.

"Grandad!" the boy groaned. That must be the new person's name, I decided. He was "Grandad" and the boy was "Tyler."

"No harm in asking," Grandad said.

"You're embarrassing her. And me. Geez, Grandad. Look, Mona, this box has Grandad's trophies. He used to be a track star in college. I could put them up on this bookshelf. Want me to?"

"Long, long ago," Grandad said, chuckling. "Sure, put them up there." Tyler began pulling clumps of paper out of a box. He pulled the paper off bright, shiny statues and began arranging them on a shelf. Mona came over to help, her face still hot.

Tyler dropped a wad of paper on the floor, and I shook myself and jumped down from the bed. Grandad's room had carpet on the floor, and it felt rough and prickly against my sore feet. I shook them out, one after the other, but it didn't help much.

"Oh, Toby, what are you doing?" Mona laughed. "You look so funny!"

Even though my feet were bothering me, the crunchy, rustling paper was so interesting I put that aside for a moment. The paper didn't need to be chased—it just lay there. Still, those noises it made! Exciting! I stalked toward a clump, crouched low, paused to make sure it wasn't about to run away, and leaped. Once I had my teeth in the paper, I shook it hard, and it made more of that noise. I growled to show it who was boss.

Tyler and Mona laughed. Grandad chuckled.

"Tyler's going to be a track star, too," he told Mona. "Following in his grandfather's track shoes!"

"Yeah, well . . ." Tyler's voice trailed away as a woman came into the room, wearing jeans and a jacket.

"Dad, how about heading down to the cafeteria for lunch?" she asked.

"Sure thing, sure thing. Hey, this lovely young lady

helping with my trophies is Mona. She's a dog trainer, so I hear."

"Hi," Mona mumbled.

"Well, nice to meet you." The woman went to a sort of metal cage that was against the wall and brought it over to the bed for Grandad. I had started to learn that people in my new home leaned on these cages sometimes when they walked. But they could go in and out of the cages as they pleased, so the cages were not like the pen where I'd once lived with my mother. People, I was already starting to learn, can do many things that dogs cannot.

"We'll just finish up the trophies," Tyler said. "I'll come after you in a minute."

The woman and Grandad left the room. I stayed with Tyler and Mona and the paper balls.

"So you run, too?" Mona asked, setting the last trophy in its place.

Wrestling with the papers had tired me out. I flopped down on the floor. It was a relief to get my itchy paws off the prickly carpet. I didn't have the energy to chew on them at the moment. I closed my eyes again.

"Yeah . . . kind of." Tyler sounded worried. I opened one eye for a quick peek at him, but I could not see any threat, so I closed it again.

"The thing is, I'm not good at it, really," Tyler went on. "I get tired so quickly. But Grandad likes the idea of me running, so I don't really tell him . . . Anyway. Want to come to lunch with us?"

"Um. Maybe another time?" I felt Mona reach down and scoop me up. I didn't even open my eyes as I snuggled deeper into the warmth of her soft T-shirt. "Toby's so calm right now, there's someplace I want to take him. I'll see you later, okay?"

Mona carried me out into the hallway, where she went one way and Tyler walked off in the other direction. I drifted off to sleep as she carried me and stirred when I could tell that she had stopped moving.

"Toby? Wake up, little guy," she whispered to me.

I could smell that we were in a different part of my home, a place I had not explored yet. Everything here was very quiet. When I opened my eyes, I could see that there were no people in chairs sitting in the hallways. Nobody was walking around using the metal cages or the long sticks they called canes.

There was a new smell in the air. My nose twitched. I did not know what this smell was, but it was different from anything else I had ever encountered. It did not smell delicious, like something to eat. It did not smell harsh enough to make my nose sting, like the water that people used here to wash the floors. It did not smell as if it needed digging, like the dirt and grass outside, or as if it needed chasing, like other furry animals.

It smelled . . . quiet. That was all I could think of. And that quiet smell was all around.

"This is the hospice wing, Toby," Mona told me. Her voice was quiet, too.

She began walking up and down the hallway with me. Sometimes we passed open doors. Each room had a bed. People were lying in some of the beds. They were very quiet, too.

"People come here when . . . when it's their time, Toby," Mona told me. "My mom explained it to me. It's not as sad as you think, really. It's a peaceful place. Families can be together while they're waiting for the end."

She walked a little, while I lay in her arms.

"I just wanted you to see this, to start getting used to it. You're going to do good work here, Toby. I know it," Mona told me. She kissed the top of my head. "It's not just how calm you are. It's the way you love people. You love everybody you meet, and that's what the people here need."

I yawned.

"Sleepy little puppy." She hugged me. "Okay, I'll take you back to bed."

The bed that Mona carried me to was a round cushion in a small room near the front desk. There were shelves in that room, with boxes and containers on them, and people came in and out all day to get what they needed. There was a bowl of water there, too, and another for food, and Mona would make sure they were both filled up before she rubbed me behind my ears and kissed me and went away for the night.

That was the strange thing, though. She always went away for the night.

As my new home grew quiet around me, someone would turn out the light in my little room, and I would lie there in the dark, wondering where Mona had gone. What about her mother, Patsy? What about the new boy, Tyler, and Grandad? Or even Fran, who sometimes frowned at me and almost never smiled?

With no people and no treats and no fascinating new smells to distract me, this was the time when my feet itched the most. I lay in my bed and gnawed at them as I thought about all the people I had met in my new home.

Which one did I belong to? Who was my new human family?

At first, I'd thought I belonged with Mona and to her mother, Patsy. That seemed to make sense. They were the ones who'd taken me away from the Ranch and my mother. They spent the most time with me, and I always felt love in their hands and heard it in their voices.

But they went away and left me at nighttime, and I was sure that a family was not supposed to do that.

What about all the other people? What about Tyler

and Grandad? What about Fran? Did I belong to them? I lay in the dark and thought and thought, and I couldn't understand.

Night after night, I chewed harder and harder, nibbling on the tough, leathery pads of my feet, tugging with my teeth at the tufts of hair that grew between my toes. It didn't make the itching go away, but I couldn't stop.

One night, a few days after Mona had taken me on a visit to the Quiet Place, I chewed so hard that I tasted blood.

Now my feet didn't just itch. They hurt. But I still couldn't stop my teeth from gnawing on them. Blood dribbled onto the pillow that I slept on, and I wondered if Mona or Patsy or Tyler would be angry about that. People didn't seem to like things that spilled on the floor. Every time I left a puddle, someone would fuss over it and come and wipe it up and hustle me outside.

But no one was here to do that now.

I wished my mother were nearby, to curl up around me. I wished Mona were here, with her gentle hands, or Patsy, or Tyler. I wished I were not alone.

I whimpered a little bit, but no one was there to hear me.

5

 In the morning, I found out that I'd been right. People did get upset about the blood on my bed. Patsy cried out in worry when she came in to see me, and she called to other people, and they clustered around. Someone took my bed away to be washed, and Patsy wrapped long white bandages around my front feet.

Fran came and watched, too. She stood a little way off. "What's wrong with the dog?" she asked.

"I don't know," Patsy answered as she taped the white wrappings securely around my paws. "Why would he do that to his feet? He must have been chewing on them all night!"

Fran made a sound like *hummmph* in her throat.

I did not like the things Patsy had wrapped around my feet! They snagged on the carpet and made me skid on the tiles. More than once, all four paws slipped out from under me and I ended up on my belly. Sometimes people laughed. Sometimes they came and helped to pick me up.

But even worse than that, the bandages kept me from chewing on my feet. My pads itched and itched and itched inside the wrappings, but I could not get at them! It was so frustrating that I limped back to the little room where I slept at night. My bed was back where it belonged, but it did not smell right. It had a harsh, soapy smell that I did not like at all. I rolled and squirmed around, trying to fix the problem, and then I lay down and put all my effort into getting those pesky things off my feet.

People kept coming in to look at me. "No, Toby," they'd say. "Leave the bandages alone, Toby." Sometimes they tried to pull my mouth away from my feet.

I'd lick their hands to show that I still liked them, but I was busy. I had a job to do.

"Oh, Toby, don't!" Mona cried out when she came into the room. "You'll make it worse. Oh, poor thing. Mom, what's wrong with him?"

"I don't know," Patsy said from the doorway. "But I got him an appointment at the vet's this afternoon. We'll figure it out, honey."

Mona filled up my food and water dishes, but I was not very interested. I just wanted to get at my feet so I could bite them and stop the itching.

Mona sat next to me and said my name a lot. "Oh, Toby. Oh, Toby," she murmured. I gave her as much attention as I could spare. I could tell she was unhappy, too.

Maybe her feet itched and ached like mine did.

That afternoon, Mona picked me up and carried me to a car. She sat in the back seat with me, and Patsy drove, just like the time they had come to get me and taken me away from the Ranch to my new home.

Were we going to a different home now? I wasn't sure how I felt about that idea. It was always great to meet new people and discover new smells, but I'd miss Tyler and Grandad and some of the other people.

I couldn't give it much thought, though. I was tired from no sleep all night and tired of my feet burning inside their bandages. With a long sigh, I lay flat on Mona's lap.

"Oh, Mom," she said, and her voice vibrated with anxiety. "Something's really wrong."

"I know, honey," Patsy said from the front seat of the car. "I know."

I did not like the new place they took me to. It smelled of harsh chemicals and cleanness and fear. A lot of dogs had been here, and they had not liked it at all.

Mona carried me to a small room with a metal table in the middle of it. I was so tired and discouraged that I lay down flat on the tabletop, even though it was hard and cold. It did feel good on my paws, though. I tugged at a strip of bandage with my teeth. I'd almost gotten it undone!

After a little while, a man with a white coat came into the room. He talked to Patsy, and then he came over to me.

"Let's see what's wrong, boy," he said to me.

His scent was very strange. I could smell that he'd petted lots of other dogs before me and most of them had been scared. A clean, chemical odor clung to his clothes, instead of something comforting, like dirt. But he talked to me kindly and his hands were gentle, so I wagged the tip of my tail a little.

He seemed to understand what the problem was, because the first thing he did was to take the bandages off my feet! Wonderful! My paws were so sore, though, that the moment I started nibbling on them, I yelped with pain.

"What could make him do that?" Patsy asked, worried.

The man checked all my feet. I followed his hands with my nose and tongue. "Well, I'll have to do some bloodwork to be sure," he said, "but I have an idea. I think Toby may have a gluten allergy."

"Can dogs get that?" Patsy asked, surprised.

"It's rare, but it does happen," the man answered. "And it can cause itchy skin, especially on the paws, just like we're seeing here. Ever since this little guy started eating dog food instead of nursing, he probably hasn't been feeling well at all."

"Oh no," Patsy said. "I had no idea!"

"There was no real way you could have been able to tell," the man told her. "It's a tricky thing to diagnose. Let me wrap Toby's paws back up so he won't make them worse, and then I'll take a blood sample."

It turned out that the man had not understood at all how to help me, because he wrapped my paws back up in more of that frustrating bandage, and then he poked me with a thin, sharp stick! I yipped from the pain and confusion. Why was he doing all this to me?

"Oh, poor Toby," Mona said, and she picked me up and held me as soon as the man let me go. Patsy had to do more talking with the man and some other people. People seem to like doing that a lot, instead of more interesting things like running or smelling or chasing or chewing. But Mona held me and cuddled me gently, which made me feel a little better.

Not much, though.

Finally, we got into the car again. Mona held me on

her lap some more as I got my teeth into a bandage and yanked.

"I just feel so bad," she said. "We should have realized something was wrong with him. All this time, he's been so unhappy!"

I let go of the bandage and looked up at her. Drops of water were sliding down her cheeks. I squirmed around so that I could reach her face and lick the water off her chin. It tasted salty and sad.

Mona was sad.

I felt sorry for her. I knew how it felt to be sad. I licked her some more and leaned against her, tucking my head under her chin. Just like my mother, Sadie, had comforted me with her touch once, I tried to comfort Mona.

"Oh, Toby. You're so sweet," she said.

"That's what's so wonderful about dogs," her mother said. The car stopped, and Patsy reached an arm back to stroke my head. "His allergies were awful, but he doesn't hold any kind of a grudge, does he? He's trying to tell you not to feel bad. He's forgiven us already. Wouldn't the world be a better place if people forgave each other as easily as dogs do?"

Over the next few days, Mona spent a lot of time with me. Patsy did, too. They talked to me and petted me, which I liked very much. What I did not like was the way they kept fixing the tape on my bandages whenever I finally managed to get it loose. I could tell they were trying to help me, but they just didn't understand that what I needed was to get those bandages off!

Mona started putting a different kind of food in my bowl, too, which was even tastier than the last kind. She talked to me while I ate it, and that was nice. "Good boy, Toby. This will help," she'd say. "That's right. You'll be better soon."

Even though Mona and Patsy didn't understand about the bandages, my feet weren't bothering me as much as they used to. They still itched at night, but less and less during the day. Even with my feet wrapped up, I felt good enough to make my way around my home, visiting all my friends.

A few days after my visit to the strange man who had poked me with the sharp stick, I was going about my business, getting petted and licking hands and sniffing shoes, when I spotted Tyler and Grandad at the end of a long hallway.

My new friends! It felt like a long time since I had seen them. My feet were feeling particularly good that morning, so I broke into a run.

It was not easy to run down the tiled hallway on my bandaged feet! My back feet slipped out from behind me, and I ended up flopping on my belly. I got up, shook my head, and tried again, with a slower start. That worked better. Soon, I was trotting. That was good! I felt ready to run!

"Here comes Toby!" Tyler called out. He was not very far away now.

I wanted to see him so much! Eagerly, I put on speed. I was running! It was working!

"Good boy!" Grandad said. He was leaning on his metal cage and chuckling.

I aimed myself at Tyler's white sneakers and braced myself to stop. But it didn't work quite as I expected. The bandages were slippery, and I could not use my claws for grip. I skidded right into Tyler's feet, and my whole body ended up piled on his shoes. But I was so glad to see him that I didn't mind at all, especially when he sat down on the floor and petted me all over while I wagged and wiggled with happiness.

"Boy, he's full of energy today, huh?" Tyler said as I licked his chin. "Mona said his feet were getting better. Here, Toby, want to chase something?" He tugged a small, rubbery ball out of a pocket and showed it to me. "Toby, ready?"

I looked up alertly. Was the ball for me?

"Get it, Toby!"

Tyler tossed the ball. It bounced away down the hallway. Instantly, I lunged after it.

Or I tried to.

All four of my feet slid out from under me at once, and I ended up flat on my stomach on the floor. Tyler and Grandad laughed, and Tyler bent down to help me up. But I had already scrambled back to my feet. That ball was getting away from me!

With my feet skidding at every step, I still managed to get up a good amount of speed. The ball ricocheted around a corner, and I did exactly the same thing, barking as I went. "Whoops, Toby, wait up!" Tyler called from behind me.

I heard Tyler saying my name, so maybe he wanted me to go back to him. But I was not interested in going back. I was interested in chasing.

The ball bounced through an open door, and I headed after it. "Hey, watch out!" yelled a voice. Feet stepped over me. I jumped and landed with both of my front paws on the ball. They still hurt a little, but the satisfaction of getting that ball more than made up for it.

I flopped down to give the ball a good chew, and then hands I had never smelled before seized me under the belly and hoisted me into the air. The ball fell out of my mouth, and I found I was looking into a dark brown face. The man holding me had fierce eyes and bristly gray hair between his lip and his nose.

"What are you doing in here?" the man said sternly.

"This is a kitchen. No dogs allowed! You're in real trouble, buster!"

I squirmed in his hands. My ears and tail drooped. I was beginning to get the feeling that somehow, I'd done something wrong.

6

 To my surprise, the face of the man who had me in his hands broke into a smile.

"Little rascal, aren't you?" he asked. "I've heard about you. You're Toby. I'm Eddie, and this is my kitchen."

Maybe I wasn't in trouble after all? I wagged hopefully, and Eddie laughed.

He smelled delicious. I squirmed to get closer to him. I could smell butter and salt and juicy meat. My nose twitched wildly, and I realized that the scents didn't just belong to Eddie. They were all around! There was a pile of sliced-up oranges on a table with a powerful odor that was sharp and sweet all at once. Bread was toasting. Sausage was sizzling on a grill. My tail wagged faster and faster. What an astounding place I'd discovered! I liked this room! I liked Eddie! A lot!

Eddie kept laughing as he put me on the floor. I snatched up the ball before it rolled away, but then I dropped it again because Eddie held out a finger with a sticky smear on the tip. Peanut butter! Marvelous!

I heard running footsteps, and a moment later, Tyler burst into the kitchen. "I'm sorry. It's my fault. I threw the ball, and Toby ran after it."

I wagged hard for Tyler, but I couldn't stop my licking to go to him.

"No kidding!" Eddie still sounded amused. "Here you go, Toby boy. I've got something better than peanut butter. Want some bacon?"

Something dropped on the floor right in front of my nose. Something that smelled salty and meaty and amazing! I grabbed it between my teeth. It crunched. It was the best thing I'd ever tasted! Better than the dog food Mona put in my bowl. Better than the treats my other friends sometimes fed me. If this was called bacon, I knew I wanted more of it. Maybe I belonged to Eddie, since he fed me the best treats? That seemed reasonable. It would be all right with me!

"Never met a dog who didn't appreciate a piece of bacon," Eddie said. "But keep him out of the kitchen, okay?"

"Sure, okay." Tyler picked me up.

I was still busy with my bacon as Tyler carried me away from Eddie and the kitchen. A heavy door closed firmly behind us as we left. I wiggled, trying to get back to my new friend and the best room I'd ever been in, but Tyler didn't let me down.

"No way, Toby," he told me. "We'd better get you back to Mona."

Mona. I knew that name. I wagged a little for Mona and licked my chops to get all the traces of bacon that I could. Maybe I'd get another chance to visit Eddie and his bacon soon.

Tyler brought me to Mona, and then something wonderful happened. Mona held me on her lap and rubbed my tummy while her mother carefully and tenderly unwrapped the bandages from my feet.

"There you go, Toby," she said as she pulled off the last scrap of white gauze. "All better. Set him down, Mona. Let's see him go!"

Running! Running was so fantastic!

It was great that my new house was so big. There was a stupendous amount of space! I tore up and down the hallways, skidding on the tile. Mona and Patsy wanted to play, too. They chased me, and I barked with joy.

Fran came out of her office, her hands on her hips, as I dashed by. "What is all this racket?" she asked. "What happened to our calm little puppy?"

I didn't hear if Mona or Patsy said anything to her in reply. I was too far ahead.

Mona caught up to me at last and went outside with me so that we could play some more. We played that game over and over for the next few days. I'd run down the hallways and Mona would chase me and take me outside once she caught me. Sometimes other people played, too. Patsy did often. Tyler did, too. Once Eddie even joined in. I let him catch me quickly because I thought he might have more bacon, but he didn't. Oh well. Maybe next time.

When we played, I'd dodge in and out of rooms and jump on beds or chairs. Sometimes there were people on the beds or in the chairs. Most of them laughed. A few gasped with surprise. Often, they wanted to pet me, and I'd let them for a little while, but then I would wiggle out from under their hands and start running again so that everybody would chase me some more. It felt like the games I'd played back in the pen with my brothers and sisters. So much fun!

A few days after my bandages came off, Mona and I were playing chase when I darted into a room and leaped upon the bed. "Well, hello there, boy!" said a person who was lying on the bed, with glasses on his face and a book propped up in front of him.

It was Grandad! I knocked his book out of his hands and licked him all over his face.

"Oh, I'm so sorry," Mona said, gasping and running into the room behind me. "He's got so much energy ever since those bandages came off. He keeps getting away from me."

"No problem," Grandad said as he petted me warmly. "Nice to have somebody who's this happy to see me."

"Hey there," said a woman sitting on a chair across the room. She shook her head and laughed. "Tyler and I are always happy to see you!"

This woman had said Tyler's name. And she smelled a little like Tyler. That was interesting. I jumped off the bed and went over to sniff at her feet and legs.

"Toby doesn't nag me about getting on that tread-mill," Grandad said, picking up his book again.

"Now, Dad, please . . . ," the woman said. "Just five minutes a day."

"I'm not a runner anymore," Grandad said, and he sounded grumpy. "Running is for tracks and trails. Out-side. Not on some kind of machine indoors. Where's Tyler, anyway? How's he coming with *his* running?"

I heard the woman in the chair say something, but a cart rattling by in the hallway was more interesting to me. Carts often had fascinating things on them; I was beginning to learn that. Sandwiches. Mashed potatoes. Macaroni and cheese. Wiggly bits of Jell-O. I dashed to the door, ready to investigate, but Mona snatched me up before I could get there.

"No way, Toby. You come with me!" she said, and she took me outside.

That was the start of something Mona called training.

Training meant that Mona would sit on the grass beside me and hold a crunchy treat in her hand. "Sit, Toby!" she'd say and press on my rear end until my legs folded up underneath me.

Or she'd say, "Down, Toby!" and tug gently on my front legs until I was stretched out on the grass.

Then I'd get the treat. That was really the only fun part.

Honestly, I thought we could find some better games to play. But I liked Mona and I liked the treats, so I went along with it.

Or I went along with it as long as one of my friends didn't walk out of the doors to join us on the lawn. Then I'd have to run over and greet the new person and see what smells he or she had brought. Or as long as a squirrel didn't try to climb up one of the trees near the fence, in which case I'd need to chase that squirrel and prop my front legs up on the tree and bark and bark.

Sometimes Tyler came outside to play Training, and Eddie came to watch now and then as well. Once, Eddie sat down on the grass with us, and I instantly burrowed into his lap, sniffing up all the delicious smells that clung to his skin and his clothing. Eddie smelled better than anyone I had ever met.

Eddie laughed and took some of the treats from Mona. "Let's see if I can get in on this training," he said.

Mona sat down on the grass to watch us.

Eddie told me to sit. I did. Then he gently pushed on one of my shoulders until I felt a little bit off balance. I lifted one paw to steady myself.

"Shake!" Eddie said. He took my lifted paw in his hand. Then he gave me a treat.

Crunch! I snapped it up. I liked treats. I liked Eddie.

We did that game a few more times, until I got impatient for the treat. When Eddie said, "Shake!" I didn't wait for him to push on my shoulder. I just picked up my paw and put it into his hand.

"Good boy!" Eddie gave me a treat right away. "Smart little thing, isn't he? He's going to be a great dog to have around the place."

"Maybe," Mona said with a sigh. "If he can figure out Stay."

"He can't do stay? Let's see. Give it a try," Eddie said.

Mona got up. She had a treat hidden in her fingers. I could smell it. A little drool dripped from my chin as I thought about how much I wanted that treat.

"Sit!" Mona told me.

I'd figured that one out. I put my rear end on the grass. My tail beat against the ground.

But Mona did not give me the treat! How unfair.

"Stay!" she said, and she took a step backward. Then another.

Whatever "stay" meant, the important issue was that I wanted that treat! And I wanted Mona! I wanted to play with her and lick her and feel her fingers scratching along my back or rubbing my ears. Why should I just sit and do nothing when I could be with a girl like Mona?

I jumped up and barked and ran to her, wagging wildly, jumping up to put my feet on her knees and pant up into her face and remind her that I was here and needed to be played with and given a treat.

"Oh, Toby!" She sighed. She did not give me the treat.

But I didn't mind too much. I'd just spotted a wiggly line of gray fur zipping up a tree on the far end of the lawn.

A squirrel! Squirrels were meant to be chased! I dashed off, barking, as fast as I could go. I could hear Eddie chuckling behind me.

Running over the grass was wonderful. Eating treats with Mona and Eddie was wonderful. Training was not so wonderful, but I didn't really mind.

I was just glad to be outside in the soft grass with

that scent I remembered from the Ranch in my nose. The smell of fresh growing things and warm dirt and quickly moving air.

The smell of running.

7

After Mona and I had played Training, she left for the day. That night, Patsy fed me and petted me good-bye. Once she'd left, I lay still in my bed for a while, but I couldn't go to sleep. So I got up and stretched and wandered to the door of my room.

I pushed at it with one of my paws, and it swung open.

Outside, the hallway was dark and quiet. It wasn't like it was in the daytime, with people walking up and down, some briskly and quickly on their own feet, some slowly in those tall cages they called walkers. There were no carts rattling by and no people in chairs. In fact, there was nobody in sight.

All that running today in the grass outside had made

me remember the Ranch and how I used to sleep in a pile with all my brothers and sisters, cuddled close to my mother's side. I didn't feel like sleeping alone. Why should I, when I had so many friends?

I trotted down the halls until I reached a familiar room. Grandad's. The door was open a crack. I stuck my nose into the crack so that I could sniff up Grandad's smell. That made the door open wider. So, naturally, I went inside.

Grandad was lying in his bed, with a light on over his head. He had a book propped up on his chest. When the door opened, he glanced over and smiled.

"Hey there, Toby boy," he said.

I wagged to hear my name and the affection in his voice. I knew I was welcome, so I hopped up on the end of his bed, turned in a circle a few times, flopped down next to his feet, and sighed with contentment.

"You telling me it's time to turn out the light?" Grandad said. He put the book on a bedside table and reached up to touch the lamp next to him. The light vanished. He shifted and settled in the bed, and I waited until he was lying still. Then I wiggled closer so that his feet would keep me warm.

It felt better to sleep like this than all alone in my bed. Did that mean I belonged to Grandad now?

It didn't seem quite right. I liked Grandad, and I was happy to be curled up next to his feet, but he wasn't the one who fed me. Mona and sometimes Patsy did that. And they both petted me and praised me, and Mona took me outside to the lawn to do the training game.

But then they left. That happened every day. They left, and I stayed.

Tyler did the same thing. He played with me, and then he left.

Grandad didn't leave. He stayed.

And there was Eddie, of course. He fed me bacon. My tail twitched a little at the thought. But it didn't seem likely that I belonged to Eddie. I didn't even see him every day, although I was happy whenever I did.

I liked my new home, I really did, especially now that my feet felt better and I could run all I liked. But it was confusing. There were so many people here. Mona and Patsy. Grandad and Tyler. Eddie and Fran. Which one did I belong to?

I fell asleep wondering.

In the morning, Grandad stirred and I wiggled up to lick his face. Someone knocked on the door. "Come in!" Grandad called sleepily, pushing me back with one hand and patting me with it at the same time.

"Excuse me. Have you seen—Toby! There you are!" Mona came in. "I'm so sorry. Did he bother you?"

"No, no, don't be sorry," Grandad said. "I enjoyed the company."

Mona scooped me up. "Toby, I'm taking you out. And then we're going to work on something new!"

Mona took me outside to squat. Then she brought me back inside and filled up my bowl. Once I'd eaten, she clipped a leash onto my collar. "Come on, Toby. New lesson today."

She took me into a room I hadn't been in before. There was a bed in it, and someone was lying in the bed.

I perked up as I sniffed, smelling a familiar person. Patsy!

"Okay, Toby, get on up," Mona said. "We know you can do it."

She patted the bed, and I jumped up beside Patsy.

"Down, Toby," Mona said. She took a treat out of her pocket. We were doing Training? That was very strange. Why were we doing Training on a bed?

But that treat smelled very interesting, so I did it. I lay down.

"Good boy, Toby," Mona said. She gave me the treat. Excellent!

"Good. Now try Lie Still," Patsy said.

Patsy! I'd been so busy with the treat that I hadn't greeted her properly. I jumped up and threw myself across her body to get to her face. I licked her cheeks and her chin and under her neck to show her how much I liked her.

She pushed me back with one hand. "No, Toby. No!" she said sternly.

I sat down in astonishment. *No?* Why was she saying no? I was beginning to learn that word, along with the other ones Mona used in training, and I did not like it. It was even worse than "stay." Why would anyone say no to licking?

A striped blanket was covering Patsy's legs and feet. I pounced on it and grabbed it in my teeth, giving it a good shake. Once Patsy saw that I was ready to play, she wouldn't say "no" anymore. We'd have fun!

"Toby, no!" Mona said. I paused with the blanket still gripped between my teeth.

Both of them saying no? What was going on here?

"Toby, lie still," Mona said, reaching out for me.

I dropped the blanket, jumped away from her hands, and leaped off the bed. If Patsy did not want to play with the blanket, I'd find something else! I tore off toward the small room with my bed.

Beside the bed was a basket of balls and toys. Good for chewing and also for chasing. I grabbed a rubber ring and trotted back to the room where I'd left Mona and Patsy.

Now we could play! I jumped up on the bed and showed Patsy the toy. She sighed. "Oh, boy. This really isn't working out."

I dropped the ring on the blanket next to Patsy, but

for some strange reason, she did not play with it. She just lay there. Was there something wrong with her? Had she been chewing on her feet?

"What's this?" asked a new voice from the doorway. We all looked that way. Fran was standing there. She was frowning. Again.

"Training," Patsy said, sitting up.

I picked up the chew toy and offered it to Patsy again. Surely she'd figure it out this time!

Fran shook her head. "You can't train a beagle not to be a beagle," she said.

It was not actually that much fun on the bed since Patsy kept ignoring the toy. I jumped off. Mona tried to grab me, but I dodged her hands and ran past Fran's feet. Then Mona and I had a great game of Chase up and down the hallways.

I loved playing with Mona.

But Mona wasn't there all the time. Patsy was usually around in the day, but often, she sat in a chair at a desk and tapped away on a plastic keyboard that did not even smell interesting. When she did that, she shooed me away. "Not now, Toby. I'm working," she'd say.

I soon came to understand that *working* meant "no fun."

Luckily, there were other people to see. I visited Grandad a lot, and sometimes Tyler was there, too. As I trotted up and down the halls, I got to know others.

There was one big room with several windows where there were soft couches and comfy chairs that got a lot of sunlight. That was a good room to visit. People were usually sitting on the couches, watching a black plastic box that blared out sound and showed moving pictures. I sniffed at it a time or two, but the pictures did not smell, so I knew that they were not real.

Frankly, I did not understand why people liked to look at that thing so much when they could have been chasing a ball or chewing a stick or petting a dog. But people are funny like that.

When I trotted into that room, there was always someone who would pet me or invite me to sit on the couch beside him or her. Some of my friends started keeping treats in their pockets for me, which of course made me even more interested in saying hello to them.

One woman was almost always there. She sat in a particular corner of the couch and didn't say much to anyone.

"Dorothy, wouldn't you like to come down the hall to the craft session?" people would say, stopping to talk to her. "Dorothy, isn't it time for your physical therapy?" "Dorothy, what if I take you outside in your wheelchair?"

That's how I figured out that her name was Dorothy. People used her name with her just like Mona used my name with me when we were doing Training.

I wondered if those people were trying to train Dorothy. She didn't look as if she enjoyed it much more than I did. They probably needed to feed her better treats.

Dorothy didn't usually answer the people. She didn't seem to talk very much. But she would say my name when I came by and reach down to rub behind my ears.

Her fingers were not very strong, but they were gentle and knew just the right spots. I'd sit down beside her and lean my head into her hand.

One day, when I came for my usual visit, Dorothy showed me something in her hand.

A ball! A small rubber ball. My tail began to swing back and forth. Balls were for chasing.

"You like that, don't you, little Toby?" Dorothy said very quietly. "All right, then."

She threw the ball for me.

It did not go very far. It hit a wall and rolled a little distance, and then bounced weakly off a chair with wheels. "Oh my!" said the person in the chair.

I chased the ball down, but it was so close by that I actually ran too far and had to skid to a stop, turn around, and grab it in my mouth.

Triumphantly, I brought the ball back to Dorothy.

Dorothy threw it for me a few more times. It wasn't like chasing a ball outside with Mona. Mona could throw a ball so that it went nearly all the way across the lawn. When Dorothy did the throwing, the ball only went a short distance. Once, I had to chase it under the legs of a table. More than once I dodged around a few people pushing those odd half cages that Grandad liked to use. All of that slowed me down.

But I got the ball each time and brought it back to Dorothy. Then I licked her shoes to say good-bye and hurried off to see some more of my friends.

Patsy was standing in the door of the room when I went back out into the hallway. "Well, look at that!" she murmured to herself. She was smiling.

After that, Dorothy usually had the little ball with her when I came by to visit. She got better and better at throwing it, too. It was more fun to chase it when she could put more power behind the throw.

It still bounced off chairs and walls and zigzagged under tables, though. More than once, I had to burrow under the couch to get it and return it to Dorothy's hand. I always found it, though. That ball could not escape me!

A few weeks after I'd first gotten to know Dorothy, she surprised me a little. When I came to visit her, she was not sitting in her usual corner of the couch. Instead, she was in one of the chairs with wheels.

Patsy happened to come into the room. "Hi, Dorothy," she said cheerfully. "Do you want to throw the ball for Toby today? I know he looks forward to it!"

"Outside," Dorothy said briefly. "I want to throw the

ball for Toby outside. In the grass. Where he can really run."

I could see surprise in Patsy's face and the way her body stiffened just for a moment. Then she smiled.

"What a superb idea," she said. "Toby will love that. Come, Toby!"

Mona had taught me Come. I knew that it meant I was supposed to stick close to the person who said it, and there would be a reward. So I stayed right at Patsy's heels as she pushed Dorothy in the rolling chair. Together we headed out onto the lawn.

The lawn! I loved the lawn. I raced in a quick circle. I figured that was not against the rules of Come, since I went right back to Patsy. I waited for my treat.

Instead, Dorothy threw the ball.

Excellent! This was nearly as good as a treat! There was so much more room for the ball to go, bouncing and rolling over the grass. Dorothy had gotten better and better at throwing it, too. I tore after it joyfully. It was more fun when I didn't have to dodge around feet and beneath tables, when I could just run and run with all the speed my paws were capable of.

"What a throw!" Patsy said when I snatched the ball in midair and swerved to bring it back to Dorothy in her chair. "Good boy, Toby!"

I knew I was a good boy. Chasing was good. Running

was good. Catching the ball and bringing it back was extremely good.

I dropped the ball at Dorothy's feet, wagging so hard that my whole rump wiggled. Dorothy leaned down to pick up the ball and threw it again.

8

Dorothy and I played outside most days after that. My favorite game, though, was running down the hallways. Sometimes Mona played with me. Sometimes Patsy did. Every now and then, Eddie joined in. It was always sensational.

Fran never played. But sometimes she watched. I wished she'd take part. She never smelled very happy, and a good game of Chase would probably make things better.

But one day Fran came to find me where I was having a quick snooze on the couch next to Dorothy. She clipped a leash on my collar and told me to come with her.

I heard "Come," so I hopped off the couch and followed Fran. But she didn't know how to do Training right. She did not give me a treat or even any petting or praise for walking by her side.

She took me to a room with a desk in it. On the desk was one of those plastic boxes that Patsy sometimes stared at. Fran sat down in a chair and waited.

I waited, too. It was dull. I sniffed along the carpet, but nothing smelled like food. I checked a wastebasket under the desk, but Fran made a disapproving grunt and pushed me away with her foot.

It only smelled like paper, anyway. Paper is not much fun to chew. So I was very happy when Patsy and Mona walked into the office a short time later. They understood playing much better than Fran did.

Except that they seemed to have forgotten, because the three of them just stood there and looked at each other and said words. Lots of words.

Humans like to do this almost as much as they like to stare at boxes with pictures on them.

"The dog is not working out," Fran said firmly.

Mona gasped. "Toby?"

I looked up hopefully and wagged harder. She'd said my name. Playing? Soon? Treats, maybe?

But she didn't even look at me.

"He tears up and down the halls like this is a

racetrack," Fran said. "Yesterday, I saw him running around the hospice ward! The people there need peace and quiet and comfort. Not a steeplechase!"

"Eddie and I grabbed him right away," Mona said.

Fran was frowning. "That's not the point."

Whatever they were talking about, it didn't seem to involve me. Or a ball to throw. But when there's nothing to play with, a dog can always improvise. Fran had let my leash drop, and I wandered away from her and jumped up on a small couch in a corner of the room.

"I think he's calming down a lot," Mona said nervously.

"And all the residents love him," Patsy added. "I see them brighten up when he walks into a room. Did you know that Dorothy goes outside to throw the ball for him nearly every day? I couldn't get her engaged in anything before this. All she wanted was to watch television. She hardly talked to anyone. Now she's going outside daily! Because of Toby."

"That hardly makes up for all the disruption," Fran said. "And can you get him off my couch, please?"

There were two soft cushions on the couch. I grabbed at one and sank my teeth into it deeply. It was just the right size to shake hard. I shook. Stitches ripped.

"Toby! No!" Mona wailed. She tried to grab the cushion from my hand.

Excellent! Tug! I loved Tug! I jumped down, braced

my feet in the carpet, and did my best to resist as Mona tried to drag the cushion from my mouth. I wouldn't let her! I was going to win!

But then Mona very unfairly worked her fingers into my mouth to force my jaws open and snatched the pillow away from me.

Mona threw the cushion back on the couch, sat down on the floor, and picked me up, holding me on her lap. I could feel that she was worried, but I couldn't see why. We'd play another game soon.

"The point is, he's not trainable," Fran said. "I gave this every chance, but he's a young beagle, and he's got way too much energy. He's not safe. He's going to knock someone over or make them trip, the way he tears through the hallways. No. It's not working out, and there's nothing left to try. Take an ad out in the paper, online, whatever. We have to get rid of this dog."

Mona gasped as if something hurt her. She held me tightly to her chest. It was not very comfortable, but I could tell she needed me, so I didn't struggle. I did squirm around so I could lick her chin.

"Get rid of Toby?" she asked. "You can't! You just can't!"

She'd said my name! I loved Mona. I licked harder.

"Mona," Patsy said. "Bring Toby and come with me."

Mona and Patsy went back into the little room that smelled like Patsy. Mona sat down on the floor and cuddled me close. "We can't just get rid of him!" she wailed, and a few tears slipped down her face. They tasted salty. "He hasn't done anything wrong!"

"I know he hasn't," Patsy said. She sounded sad, too. I would go over and lick her face soon. That would help. "Fran does have a point, though, Mona. We thought he was a calm, easygoing puppy when we got him. But the truth is he wasn't well. Thank goodness we figured that out and helped him. But now—well, he's a beagle. And beagles love to run."

"If we could just take him home . . . ," Mona said.

"You know we can't. No pets. It's the apartment rule."

"I know." Mona wiped her face. "But Fran's not right about the training. Toby's really smart. He picks things up so quickly."

"Except Stay. Or Lie Still," Patsy said gently.

My ears drooped at the sound of those words. We weren't doing Training *now*, were we?

"If I just had a little more time, I could teach him!" Mona said. "Please, Mom. He's such a good dog."

I wagged. I liked being a good dog.

Patsy sighed. "I'll do what I can, Mona. But don't get your hopes up. I can drag my feet a little about putting out an ad, but Fran's the boss here. If she says Toby has to go, there's nothing either you or I can do."

The next morning, when I went to see Dorothy,

Patsy and Mona were already there. "Of course I'll try," I heard Dorothy say. "Anything for Toby."

I raced up to Dorothy, who was sitting in her wheelchair. But we didn't go outside! I watched, puzzled, as Patsy helped Dorothy move out of the wheelchair and sit on the couch.

I looked all over for the little ball. I did not see it anywhere.

Mona patted the couch next to Dorothy. "Up here, Toby."

I jumped up and sniffed at Dorothy's lap. Was the ball there?

"Toby, sit!" Mona told me. I sighed and sat. *Oh well. If I must.*

"Down," Mona said. I reluctantly slid on my belly right next to Dorothy. Training was not anywhere near as fun as chasing the ball.

"Now, lie still, Toby. Lie still!" Mona said. She backed up a few steps. It seemed as if she were holding her breath.

Dorothy's soft, gentle hand touched my head and stroked all the way down my back.

I wagged once. Then I hopped up and stuck my whole head under one of the cushions. Maybe the ball was here? Since Dorothy seemed to have forgotten it, I figured it was my job to remind her.

"Toby, no!" Mona said. I pulled my head out from

under the cushion and looked at her in surprise. *No?* Why was she saying no?

She told me to sit and lie down again. I did it. Why did Training mean having to do things so many times?

"Lie still, Toby," Mona told me. I looked up at her hopefully. When were we going to play?

"Okay," Mona whispered. "We won't make him do it for too long. Just a few seconds more . . ."

Suddenly, I had an idea. My ears twitched with the excitement of it. Maybe the little ball was lost! Maybe that was why we weren't playing with it. All I had to bring Dorothy was another toy!

I leaped off the couch and raced out of the room. Next to my bed was the basket full of toys. I dug through it and found one that I liked a lot, a braided rope with a ring at one end. With that in my teeth, I trotted back to the TV room.

Dorothy was still on the couch. Mona was sitting on it, too, looking discouraged.

I jumped up and laid the braided rope in Dorothy's lap. I'd solved the problem! Now we could play! That would definitely cheer Dorothy up. Mona, too.

"Oh, Toby," Mona groaned.

I played Lie Still with quite a few of my friends that day. Mona seemed to have forgotten the rules of the game, though, because I never got any treats.

I forgave her. I loved her very much. When she put

me in my bed before she left that night, she kissed the top of my head, and I felt so much love from her that my tail beat against my soft blankets.

"Toby, you have to do better," she whispered to me. "You've got to learn this!"

I loved hearing Mona say my name. I licked her nose. I couldn't wait to play more tomorrow.

9

 That night, I explored the halls and slept at the foot of Dorothy's bed. The next day turned out to be one of those days when Mona did not come in the morning. Patsy found me with Dorothy and took me out to the lawn so that I could pee.

Someone came to the door while I was busy doing that. "Patsy? Fran needs to ask you something," the woman called.

"Okay. Toby, I'll be right back," Patsy said. "Be good."

I wagged. It was nice to hear the word "good." I was good.

I yawned and stretched, working out the kinks in my back legs and then in my front ones. I thought about the food that would be waiting for me in my bowl. I thought about Eddie and about bacon.

Soon, I'd be eating. That was such a lovely thought, I wagged my tail. Meanwhile, I sniffed along the grass. Then I froze.

Something had moved, a nervous little twitch that had caught my attention. An animal, crouched in the grass. Now it was sitting perfectly still, but it was too late for that. I knew it was there.

Its smell drifted across the lawn to me. Not a squirrel. Something different. Something interesting.

I had to find out more.

I started across the lawn toward the new animal, and instantly, it turned and ran. It did not run like a squirrel, though, or like a dog, racing across the ground. Instead, it leaped! A giant jump took it ahead, and then it gathered its back legs under it and leaped again!

I was so surprised that I barked. Then I tore after it, my claws digging into the soft dirt and ripping up clumps of grass. I needed to catch this animal before it ran up a tree like the squirrels always did!

To my surprise, it did not head for the trees. Instead, it bounded straight into a bush that grew against the back fence. I followed close behind. Leaves whapped at my face, but I could still see the jumping animal dive into a hole in the fence, wiggle for a moment, and disappear.

I squirmed forward and put my nose into the hole. I could not fit through it like my quarry had. Not fair! I pulled my nose back and barked in frustration.

This was a problem to solve. When Dorothy had lost the little ball, I'd solved that problem by bringing her the rope. Now I had to figure out a new puzzle.

It wasn't hard. The hole was too small for me—so I would make the hole bigger!

I scrabbled at the dirt under the fence with both paws. It was damp and soft, and the hole was bigger in no time. I flung myself into it. It was a tight squeeze, but I wiggled and twisted and shoved with my back legs, and with one last effort, I was through!

Now where had that jumping animal gone? I shook dirt off my fur and looked around.

No animals. Disappointing. But I did see a sidewalk, and a road, and new trees that might have squirrels in them. And coming along the road, I saw something else.

A group of boys, all of them wearing shorts and T-shirts, all of them running.

Running! Excellent!

The boys came closer and closer, and a warm wind blew their scent to me. My head and ears lifted. They all smelled sweaty, and most of them smelled happy, but one smell in particular was familiar. Tyler was running in that group of boys!

I dashed forward to meet them. A friend! This was outstanding!

I ran in circles around the boys, barking happily. They laughed and slowed down, and Tyler got down on one knee to pet me. He was breathing in big gasps.

"Good boy, Toby," he panted. "What are you doing out, huh?"

"Come on. Gotta keep moving," one of the other boys said, and they began to run forward again. "Hey, Tyler, you coming?"

Tyler got to his feet, hesitating, looking down at me. "I should take you back," he told me. "But I've got to finish this run. Well, you like running. You want to come?"

Come! I knew that word! I jumped and wagged hard to let him know I understood.

"Okay, then," Tyler said. He began to jog forward, going a little faster to catch up with the other boys. "Come on, Toby! Stay with me!"

Running! Running with boys! It reminded me of my days at the Ranch, before my feet itched all the time. I'd run and raced with my brothers and sisters. Now I was running with people. Running outside, in the sunshine, smelling dirt and grass and sweat and people and all the other animals that had crossed our

path, smelling the freshness of air moving quickly. It was fantastic!

Sometimes I ran at Tyler's side. Sometimes I dashed ahead to lead the pack. Sometimes I had to stop to sniff a particularly interesting smell. Once I even found a piece of pizza crust lying on the ground. What a day!

When I looked up from finishing the pizza crust, I noticed that Tyler was running more slowly than the rest of the boys. He'd fallen behind the group. I raced to his side.

He looked down at me as he jogged, smiling for a second, but he didn't say much. He was breathing too hard—panting, almost. Maybe he was hot and needed to cool off.

"Tyler, you okay?" one of the other boys called back.

Tyler waved and nodded and sped up a little so that he was closer to them. But he slowed down again almost at once.

"Come on!" one of the other boys yelled.

Tyler sped up again. But pretty soon he was far behind the others, and he stopped, bending over to put both hands on his knees.

His chest heaved, and he pulled in great gusts of air.

"Hey, Tyler, want us to wait?" one of the other boys called.

Tyler shook his head. He waved at them. They kept running.

I looked at the boys, running steadily along the street. I dashed after them. Time to catch up!

Then I looked back at Tyler. He hadn't moved.

This was odd. Why didn't Tyler want to run, when running was so much fun? I circled back to him and nosed at his feet. Shouldn't he be moving?

Tyler took a few steps and sat down on the curb. "I don't think . . . I'm going to make . . . the cross-country team," he said to me, wheezing.

He had a pack on his back with a little hose that hung from it. He put the hose in his mouth and sucked on it.

"You want some water, Toby?" He held out one cupped hand and squeezed some water into it from the hose. Then he held out his hand to me, and I lapped it up.

"Good dog," Tyler told me. He was not panting so hard anymore. "You ran a couple of miles, you know that?"

He poured me more water, and I drank it eagerly. My stomach was reminding me that I hadn't had any breakfast yet, but that didn't matter. The other boys were so far ahead by now! Shouldn't we be running with them?

I hurried forward a few steps, paused, and looked back.

But Tyler didn't seem to understand that he was supposed to chase me. He sat still.

I paced a few steps. I whined, frustrated. Why were we staying in one place?

"You want to keep going, huh?" Tyler got slowly to his feet. He sighed. "Okay. Okay."

He began to run again, slowly. His feet seemed heavy. I stayed with him, even though I wanted to dash ahead, to catch up with the pack of boys moving more quickly along the road. Somehow it felt important to be near Tyler.

We hadn't gone long before we met the boys coming back in the other direction. Then I did break away from Tyler to race up to them, barking a greeting. They laughed. I headed with them to where Tyler was waiting.

We all began running together, back the way we'd come.

All of the boys were going slower now. But Tyler was the slowest of all. He fell to the rear of the pack quickly, and he stayed there. The distance between him and the runner in front of him stretched out longer and longer.

I stayed close at my friend's heels. By the time we got back to the fence, he was not going much faster than a walk.

I knew that my breakfast was waiting for me on the other side of that fence, so I barked at Tyler to let him know I had to leave. He stopped for a moment, letting the other boys pull even farther ahead, and bent down to pat me.

"Too bad . . . you can't be . . . on the track team for me . . . Toby," he wheezed.

I licked his hand and wiggled my way back under the gap in the fence.

When I got back into the yard, Patsy was calling to me from the back door. "There you are, Toby!" she said. "I couldn't see you at first. Come on in. I bet you're hungry."

Breakfast was delicious. I licked the bowl until it was shiny and drank half of my water. Then I had to consider which friend I wanted to visit first.

I decided on Grandad.

When I reached his room, he was stretched out in bed with a book, as usual. I hopped up and stuck my head between his face and the book so he would remember that my ears needed scratching. He put down the book and laughed and did his job.

I was tired from my long run with Tyler, my belly was full of breakfast, and I was happy to be with one of my friends. I curled up next to Grandad and settled down for a nap.

After I'd been asleep for a while—I didn't know

quite how long—a sound drifted into my ears. "Toby! Toby!"

It was Mona's voice. My ears twitched, awake before the rest of me. Then I woke up all the way, stood, shook, and stretched.

"Good morning to you, too, boy," Grandad said. He had put his book down on the bedside table. "You had a good snooze!"

He scratched my back, and I wiggled happily. Then I hopped off the bed to find Mona.

She was standing near the kitchen door, talking with Eddie. I could tell from the way she stood—her arms crossed tightly in front of her, her weight shifting from foot to foot—that she was worried about something.

I dashed up to her and put my front paws on her knees so I could be closer to her face. Then I dropped down, because Eddie had the best thing ever in his hand. Bacon! I did Sit at once, before she could even ask. Then I put a foot up in the air since Eddie usually told me to Shake. Then I drooled.

Eddie chuckled, but only a little, and not as loudly as he usually did. "Smart as a whip," he said. "Here, Toby. Good boy."

He dropped the bacon, and I snapped it up. Nothing was better than bacon!

"I'm sure going to miss you, Toby," Eddie said. I wagged for my name and for the chance of more bacon.

"We all are. But Fran makes the rules. And if she says you go, I guess you go."

Mona dropped her arms to her sides and looked determined. "He doesn't have to go yet. Maybe I can still train him. Yesterday was the last day of school, and it's summer vacation now. I can come all day and work with him. You just said how smart he is! Maybe I can get Fran to change her mind."

"Good luck," Eddie said, and he leaned over to pet me. I licked his fingers, which smelled and tasted so perfectly of bacon. I loved Eddie. I loved Mona and Grandad and Dorothy and Patsy, too. This home hadn't been exactly what I'd expected when I'd left my mother and Walt and the Ranch, but I was happy I was here.

"Come on, Toby," Mona said. She sounded determined.

We did a lot of Training that day.

The next morning, it was Mona who was there to let me out first thing. I gave her some licks to show how much I loved her, and then I hurried off to check the lawn for more of those bouncy animals.

I could smell that a few of them had been around earlier, but none seemed to be here now. Patsy came out to join Mona, and while they were talking, I headed for the fence.

There might be a bouncy animal on the other side of it. I forced myself under the bush and wiggled through the hole to check.

No animals, except a squirrel who chattered angrily at me from a tree high overhead. I ignored him. I was starting to learn about squirrels. There is no point chasing them once they are high up. But if they're on the ground, well, they'd better watch out!

I guess the bouncy creature had learned his lesson and wouldn't be hanging around anymore. But down the street, I spotted something that made my head and ears go up and my tail start moving.

The boys! The running boys! They were coming back. And Tyler was with them!

I dashed off to join them and ran in circles around them, barking with happiness. They laughed but didn't stop running. "Guess you're not the only newbie!" one of the boys said to Tyler as they jogged.

Tyler nodded but didn't have the breath to answer.

This was excellent. New friends! More running! I settled in by Tyler's side. Slowly, he began to fall back from the group, just like the day before.

I ran a little ahead of him. Then I looked back. Maybe he'd figured out how to play Chase Me now.

He had! He sped up just a little, so he was running not far behind my tail. We ran like that, with the boys ahead of us and the wind in my nose bringing us the good smells from all around.

I looked back again to see if Tyler needed another reminder. Apparently he did, because he'd stopped. He stood bent over, with his hands braced on his knees.

I hesitated. Should I go back to him?

But the other boys were still running. One of them turned to look at both of us.

That boy was telling me to chase him! I leaped forward and barked for Tyler so he would know what to do.

I heard him groan a little. "Okay, okay, Toby," he gasped.

He started running again.

We turned around not long after that and headed back again. I ran in a circle around the boys to say good-bye and then wiggled through the hole in the fence and crawled out from under the bush, ready for breakfast.

Mona was standing in the yard, looking worried again. I raced up to her, panting and wagging. Why was she worried when we were together? And when there was bacon in the world?

"Toby!" she said. "Where were you? I looked all over the yard and didn't find you. I even checked inside." She bent down to pet me. I was glad that she was glad to see me.

"Were you hiding somewhere? Were you, Toby?" She put her worried face close to mine. I licked her nose. Breakfast now?

She shook her head and sighed. "Weird," she muttered. And she took me indoors to feed me.

Breakfast really is wonderful.

10

After breakfast, I wandered into the room with all the couches and took another nap, this time with Dorothy. When I woke up, she had found the little ball again, so we went outside for some throwing. Once we were done with that, I went back inside and greeted all my friends. Some of them had treats for me. But when I got to Grandad's room, I found something better than treats.

Chicken.

He was sitting at a small table by the window, eating some chicken from a plate. I was so happy to see him! And his chicken, too! I sat right at his feet, waiting for him to drop a bite down to me.

I was pretty sure he was getting ready to do it when

Tyler walked in. He was walking a bit slowly, as if his legs were tired. I wagged to show him that I liked him and I was happy he was there, but I needed to stay focused on the chicken for the moment. I was sure he would understand.

"Toby?" I heard Mona call from the hallway. I wagged for her, too. But I stayed still, watching the fork move from Grandad's plate to his lips.

"Toby's in here!" I heard Tyler call. "But he's a little busy right now."

Mona came in. She laughed when she saw me, raising my head when Grandad lifted his fork, lowering it when the fork returned to the plate.

"He knows what's important," Grandad said.

"Well, I guess he's got a right to be hungry," Tyler said. "He ran a couple of miles this morning."

Mona and Grandad both looked at him in surprise.

"With the cross-country club," Tyler explained. "I figured I should tell you. He snuck out under a hole in the fence this morning, and yesterday, too, and he ran with us. He loved it!"

"I bet he did!" Mona's smile was big. "So *that's* where he was this morning. I called and called. I was getting really worried. Wait, you're on a cross-country team?"

Tyler shook his head. "No way. Not a real team. Just a club, for the summer. My mom rented an apartment up here so we can hang out with Grandad more. And

there's this club of boys who run every morning. Most of them are on the teams at their schools, staying in shape for track, you know. But they said I could tag along. It's great. Really fun."

There was something about his voice that sounded odd to my ears. I knew that word, *fun*. But Tyler's voice didn't sound happy. And people were usually happy about fun.

It was strange. Almost as strange as the fact that Grandad kept forgetting to give me some chicken.

"Oh, that's cool," Mona said. "So you're going to be visiting a lot?"

"Every day," Tyler answered her.

"I'm here every day, too." I glanced over at Mona for a moment. Her face was doing that funny thing again, where it heated up and got darker. "Training Toby. We've really got to work on his skills, or . . ."

"Yeah, I heard." Now Tyler's words and his voice were both sad. As soon as I got some chicken, I'd have to make them both feel better.

"Mona?" I heard Patsy's voice from out in the hallway. "I need you for a minute."

"Okay, Mom!" Mona called back. "I'll be back for Toby soon," she said to Grandad and Tyler. "He's got to work on Lie Still!"

I glanced at her. But it was clearly not a command, because she was already hurrying from the room.

110

I stayed, because, well, the chicken was here. Tyler sat down on the bed.

"So how is it here? Now that you're settled in and everything?" he asked.

"Pretty good. No complaints," Grandad said. "Now, I liked staying with you and your parents, but it could get a bit dull during the day. Your mom and dad at work, you at school, nobody around to talk to. Plenty of company here. That's good. Maybe I'll get a girlfriend."

At last, he dropped a bite of chicken down for me! I snapped it up. Then he put the fork down. That seemed to mean that chicken was over, but I kept an eye on the plate, just in case.

"So what about you?" Grandad asked Tyler. "That girl Mona, she's pretty great. You like her, huh?"

Tyler shrugged.

"A shrug is not an answer," Grandad told him.

"That's what Mom says," Tyler replied. He flopped down to lie on his back on the bed.

"Where do you think she got it from?" Grandad said, and he and Tyler both laughed a little. "So, Mona?"

"Yeah, all right, I like her. She's cool. You're such a nag, Grandad."

"I only nag when I'm right. Smart girl like that—pretty, too—she's not going to wait around forever. Take some advice from an old man. You need to tell her how you feel."

"Yeah, okay. Sometime." Tyler lay looking at the ceiling as if he were talking to it instead of to Grandad.

"How's the running coming? That's a great idea, that club. You'll be beating the pants off the other kids come the fall."

"Maybe," Tyler said softly.

"Maybe? For sure."

"Grandad, it's not going so good." Tyler still didn't sit up. "I'm slow. I'm the slowest on the team."

"So what?"

Tyler picked up his head and stared at Grandad. "So what? So I'm not going to win any races, that's what."

Grandad snorted. "Speed? Cross-country isn't a sprinter's game, boy. It's about determination. You can't outrun those other boys? Then you beat them with your wind."

"What does that mean?"

Grandad twisted in his chair so he was looking right at Tyler. "They run, you run a little farther. Every time. That's what it means. Pretty soon you'll be running so far that a short race will be a breeze."

Tyler sighed and let his head fall back onto the bed. "Yeah, maybe," he answered.

Tyler left Grandad's room not long after that, and Mona came back to get me for some more Training in the yard. Frankly, it was not very exciting. But things got livelier when the door opened and three kids ran out. Patsy was behind them.

"A puppy!" the youngest girl shrieked.

She was smaller than Mona, in a white dress that puffed and swirled out when she ran. There was a boy a little older, and both of them, I soon discovered, were very good at Chase Me.

The other kid, a girl who was a little older, sat down on a bench with Patsy. Patsy put her arm around the girl and talked to her gently.

"Toby!" Mona called out, a little sternly.

I stopped my chasing and looked over at her, puzzled. What did she want? Why didn't she come and play too?

"It's all right, Mona," Patsy said. "Let him run. This is part of Toby's job, too."

The two kids and I played Chase Me over the grass and around one of the big trees. Mona watched. So did the girl who was sitting with Patsy. Every now and then, that girl rubbed a hand over her face.

The littlest girl chased me around the tree, and I spun away from her. She slipped on a patch of wet earth and fell to her hands and knees. I ran back to be sure she still wanted to play, and I licked her face and chin. She giggled. I tore off again, and she jumped up to follow me with her brother right behind.

Mona had found one of the rubber balls, and she tossed it to the boy. He threw it as hard as he could, which was not very far. Even Dorothy could get it farther! But I pounced on it and brought it back, and the little kids took turns throwing it. I was so glad we'd given up Training for now. This was much better!

On one of my trips back with the ball, I caught a familiar scent and looked up to see Fran standing in the doorway. Her eyes grew wide as they looked over the group of us, playing Throw the Ball. Then they grew narrow.

"Toby! No! Bad dog!" she said.

I was so surprised that I dropped the ball. It bounced on the grass. The little boy ran to get it.

What was bad about playing? How could that be bad? My ears went down. My tail drooped.

A new man, one I hadn't seen before, was in the doorway behind Fran. She moved aside to let him come out onto the lawn with us. The tall girl, the one who'd been sitting with Patsy, ran to him, and he hugged her tightly.

Fran turned to them, and her whole body softened. Her face looked tender. I had not seen her look like this before, ever. She always looked so impatient when she looked at me.

She gently touched the girl's back and put her hand on the man's arm. I remembered my mother, Sadie, and how she had curled her body around mine when she sensed that I was hurting and needed to be comforted.

"I'm so sorry for your loss," Fran said to the man and the girl. Even her voice was gentle.

"My mom isn't suffering anymore," the man said quietly, with his arms still around the girl. "That's what's important."

The boy picked up the ball and threw it for me, and I went after it. He didn't throw it far, though, so I could still hear Fran's words. I didn't understand what they meant, but I understood the tone. She was using her voice to comfort the man, just as my mother had used her body's warmth to comfort me.

"I'm sorry about your daughter's dress, too. There's mud all over the front."

The man shrugged. "It's just mud. It doesn't matter at all. I'm so glad they're playing with the little dog. Toby, right?" I heard my name and perked up my ears as I brought the ball back to the boy. I wasn't a bad dog anymore, I felt sure. Whatever I'd done wrong, it was over.

"Honestly, Toby was one of the reasons we picked this facility for my mom's last days," the man went on. "Look at my kids. He's helping them so much. This day would have been too sad for us all without Toby. He's a great dog."

My name again! I still had the ball in my mouth, so I ran over to offer it to the man, tail wagging. I could feel and smell that he was sad. If he played a little with us, he'd feel better.

He reached down and picked the ball up with one arm still around the tall girl. Then he threw it, so hard it soared through the air, bounced off the fence, and zigzagged beneath a bush.

I dashed off after it, but I could still hear Fran's voice from behind me as I ran.

"I'm glad you like the dog. Do you want him?" she asked.

11

I brought the ball back to the man while he and Fran talked. The little kids seemed to be begging him for something, just like my brothers and sisters and I used to beg and whine for milk from my mother when we were hungry. "Please, Daddy? Can we? Please, let's take Toby!" they kept saying.

I knew they were talking about me, so I licked their ankles and knees and anything else I could reach.

"Well, I'll think about it," the man said. "That's all I can say. Today's not a good day to decide anything. But I'll give it a lot of thought."

My new friends did not stay long after that. Once they had gone, Dorothy came out in her wheelchair and threw the ball for me a few more times. That was fun. It was nice to have so many people who wanted to play.

Mona had to leave then. "Swimming lesson," she said to me. "We'll do more work tomorrow, okay, Toby? You're a good dog. You did good today with those kids."

She kissed me good-bye, and then she went away.

I wandered around to see if I could find Eddie and some bacon. No luck. But a few of my other friends had treats for me in their pockets or in little dishes next to their beds. Delicious!

I stopped by the door of a room I had not been inside very often. I did not quite understand what people did in there. Sometimes they lay on tables and pulled at ropes that were attached to heavy weights. Sometimes they perched on odd machines and turned pedals with their feet. Sometimes they even sat on the floor and moved their arms and legs around. It looked sort of like playing, but as far as I could tell, they were not having any fun.

Today, I caught a familiar scent as I stood by the door, so I hurried in to investigate. Grandad and Tyler!

Grandad was leaning on the bars of his metal cage next to a very strange contraption. There was a long, thin flat surface, sort of like a table, but only a few inches about the ground. I sniffed at it. It smelled rubbery. Some bars stuck up from one end, with handles to hold. I wondered what it was doing there and why Tyler and Grandad were both looking at it. Why do people spend so much time looking at things that they cannot play with or eat?

Grandad was frowning. His shoulders were hunched up a little. I recognized what his body was saying. He looked like I felt when Mona wanted me to do Training and I would rather play.

Tyler was standing nearby. "C'mon, Grandad," he begged.

Was Tyler trying to make Grandad do Training? He needed some treats. That would probably help.

"I've got better things to do than walk and get nowhere," Grandad said gruffly. "It's boring."

"So you're bored for five minutes," Tyler said. "Please. Mom said you have to."

"I don't have to do what your mother says, young man."

"Just five minutes."

Grandad snorted. "One minute. That's it. Then you and your mother stop pestering me."

He put the walking cage to one side. Tyler took it and moved it away a little bit. Then Grandad stepped up on to the flat, rubbery surface.

I was about to leave since no one had any treats or chicken here, but then something remarkable happened.

The surface Grandad was standing on started to move!

I was so surprised that I barked at it. Tyler laughed a little. Grandad looked down and smiled very briefly.

His feet were moving. He was walking but not going anywhere. This was very strange! I needed to find out more.

I jumped up on the black surface right behind Grandad. It moved underneath me. I stared down at it in astonishment, and then suddenly I was falling off. I plopped down onto the carpet behind the contraption as Tyler laughed more and even Grandad chuckled. He was not quite so grumpy about his Training now.

I did not like being dumped off like that. I jumped right back up behind Grandad, trying to catch up with his feet. It was hard! Every time I thought I'd made it, the surface pulled me back. Quickly, I learned that I had to keep my feet moving. If I did that, I didn't get whisked away and deposited on the carpet.

It was a little like running with Tyler and the boys, except that we weren't outside with all the good smells. Still, it was fun! Grandad was walking, and I was walking. We were walking together! I barked up at him, and he laughed.

"Good dog, Toby!" Tyler said.

"What's going on here?" asked a voice behind him.

I looked over. There was Fran. I could not spare her

much attention, though. If I stopped concentrating on my feet, I started to slide away from Grandad.

"Toby's doing the treadmill with my grandfather!" Tyler said. "They've been on there ten minutes already."

"Ten minutes? Really?" Fran said. She sounded surprised.

"Enough," Grandad said. He was starting to breathe a little heavily, just like Tyler did when we ran. The black surface under our feet slowed down and stopped.

I guess that meant we were done. I hopped off, and Grandad climbed down more slowly. Tyler had his walking cage ready for him.

"Good boy, Toby," Tyler said. "Maybe you should get on the treadmill with him every time."

"Well, it's more interesting with Toby," Grandad admitted.

After that, I did Treadmill with Grandad most days. When my other friends saw us playing, they wanted me to do Treadmill with them, too. I'd walk with lots of people, the surface moving under us. Sometimes I'd even wait by the machine until a friend came along. "Want a walk, Toby?" he or she would say and get on with me.

I liked doing Treadmill! It was almost as much fun as bringing the ball back to Dorothy or playing Chase in the halls with Mona. Sometimes Fran came to watch me. She'd stand with her arms folded as I trotted along next to my friends.

As I lay in my bed at night, though, I wondered about all the games I played. When I walked on the treadmill with Grandad, I felt like his dog. When I chased the ball for Dorothy and she stroked my ears, I was hers. When Tyler and I ran with the other boys, it seemed like I was his.

Most often, I was Mona's dog, when we did Training or played Chase. But it didn't seem right for me to belong to all these people at once.

A dog was meant to be with people; I knew that deep down. That's why we left our first families. Dogs and people were supposed to be together.

But how could I belong to one person after another? Whose dog was I, really? Grandad's or Dorothy's? Mona's or Tyler's or Patsy's?

When I lay there in the dark, these thoughts would begin to bother me as much as my feet used to. Then I'd hop up and go out into the dimly lit hallways. It could be hard to find a friend at night. The room with the couches and the black box with pictures on it was always quiet and empty. So was the treadmill room. And lots of doors were closed.

I'd wander restlessly, sniffing at each door I came to, until one or another gave way under my paw or my nose. Then I'd go in and see if a friend was inside, lying on a bed. I'd hop up and curl up in a ball near the person's feet, and after a while, I'd fall asleep.

But sleeping did not make the thoughts go away, not entirely.

Whom did I truly belong to?

Most mornings, Mona came to find me. But after the day I'd been a good dog for playing with the kids on the lawn, it was Patsy who took me out and brought me my breakfast. Then she called to me to Come.

I trotted at her heels, and we came to a room where Mona was lying on a bed. That was funny! It was my other friends, like Grandad and Dorothy, who lay on the beds. Not usually Mona. I ran up to the bed with my tail wagging. What was going on?

I could smell the clean white sheets with their soapy smell and of course the smell of Mona herself, warm and welcoming and loving. Then my tail started to beat even faster. I could smell treats, too! Mona had treats!

I jumped up on the bed and sniffed all around, trying to find them. Mona did not move.

"Lie still, Toby!" Patsy said firmly.

Where were those treats? I sniffed Mona's hands. Not there. I burrowed my nose into her clothes.

"Lie still!" Patsy pushed on my rear end so that my legs folded up under me.

That reminded me. We were playing Training, obviously. I knew about Training. I did what a person said, and then came the treats.

Treats! So exciting!

I was thinking so much about the treats that I couldn't quite remember what Patsy had asked me to do. Lie, wasn't it? I was already sitting, so I was halfway there. I stretched my front legs out flat on the bed for two seconds, and then I bounced back up. There. I'd done Lie. Treat now?

No treat. Mona still didn't move.

"He's not getting it," Patsy said with a sigh.

Something else? I was supposed to do something else. I tried Sit. I drooled a little.

Mona sighed.

I remembered Eddie's trick, and I stuck a paw up in the air. There! This time I was sure I'd done it!

But it seemed that I hadn't. The smell of the treats was all around me, making me quiver with excitement. But nobody was offering me any. And Mona still wasn't moving. Why wasn't she moving? Didn't she want to play? Was something wrong?

"Toby, lie—" Patsy started to say.

But I interrupted her. I'd remembered my last trick. Eddie had taught me this one. It was called Speak.

I barked once. Then I did it a few more times in case Mona and Patsy hadn't noticed.

The door to our room swung open, and Mona sat up on the bed. I jumped into her lap, nosing around for the treats. Was she going to keep them all for herself? So unfair!

Fran stood in the doorway, looking irritated. "Why is the dog barking?" she asked.

"We were training him," Mona said nervously. "He just got kind of confused."

"Training him? Why? You know I said he needs to go to a new home."

"We're just—" Mona began.

Patsy put a hand on her shoulder. "Mona wanted to keep working with him while we look for a new home," she said calmly to Fran.

"Did you put an ad in the paper?" Fran asked.

"Yes, I did. No one's called yet."

"Excuse me," said a voice behind Fran. "Is Toby in there?"

It was Tyler. He was wearing shorts and white shoes with thick, rubbery soles. He looked like that when we went running!

Since Mona had forgotten how to do Training properly, I jumped off the bed and dodged past Fran's high heels to sniff at Tyler's shoes. They smelled like rubber and dirt and trash and all the amazing things about outside. I loved his shoes. I licked them happily.

"Can Toby come out for a run?" Tyler asked, looking from Fran to Patsy to Mona. "If it's okay?"

"A run?" Fran looked confused.

"Yeah, he runs with me sometimes. All the boys in the club really like it when he comes. They sent me in to ask."

"So he runs with you?" Fran gave Patsy a funny look. "Would you like to keep him?" she asked Tyler.

Tyler had dropped down to one knee to greet me properly, scratching around my neck and rubbing his hands along my back. I wiggled with pleasure.

"No, I can't. We're only staying up here for the summer, to be near my grandfather. And the place where we're living says no pets. He's a great dog, though. Someday I want one like him."

"Too bad. But take him for a run, by all means," Fran said. "He seems to have plenty of energy."

Mona slipped off the bed. "I'll get his leash."

"I'll be outside stretching," Tyler said. "Thanks for letting Toby come with me." He left, and Mona called to me to go with her.

"That boy . . . he's got a crush, doesn't he?" I heard Fran say to Patsy as I followed Mona down the hall.

Mona took me outside and handed my leash to

Tyler. She didn't give me a treat for doing Come properly, though. Maybe she forgot because her heart was beating quickly and her face was hot, as if she'd been running, too.

This time, I ran with my leash on, which was a little different from before. But it was still fantastic. We passed so many trash cans, and I barked at a cat, who sped away and jumped up on the railing of a porch, and I even saw one of those bouncy animals—I'd heard Tyler calling them rabbits—darting into a bush. So exciting!

Tyler ran closer to the other boys, and I did not have to choose between sticking with the pack and staying with my friend. I liked that. When we got back, he took me in the front door and gave my leash to Mona instead of leaving me to wiggle through the hole in the fence.

Mona seemed to know what I needed. She led me straight to my water dish and watched while I gulped down half of it. It was so refreshing!

"Good run, Toby?" she asked me when I lifted up my head and shook it so that drops of water from my muzzle sprayed in all directions.

"But we have to keep training," she told me. Her voice was serious. "We don't have much time. Let's do it again. You're a smart dog, Toby. You'll get this. I hope."

I wagged for *smart dog* in case it was anything like

good dog. Mona kept my leash on and took me down the hall. Patsy was waiting for us.

"Can we go in and see Dorothy?" Mona asked her mother.

"She's not having a good day," Patsy answered. "She's in some pain. But she does want to see Toby. It's worth a try."

They took me into a room, and my friend Dorothy was lying on a bed just as Mona had been earlier.

"Hi, Dorothy," Mona said. "Do you want to see Toby? Could he lie with you a little bit?"

"Yes," Dorothy said from the bed. Her voice sounded soft.

"Well, I'm not sure how long he'll stay," Mona said. "But we'll try. He likes you."

Gently, she lifted me up and put me on the bed by Dorothy's side. I sniffed her face. She smelled tired and unhappy. I remembered how I'd felt when my feet had been so sore and all I'd wanted to do was sleep. Maybe Dorothy's feet were hurting her just like mine used to.

Her soft, gentle hand came up to rub my ears with her light touch. "Good boy, Toby," she said.

I licked at her fingers. Then I yawned. After such a long run, my legs were tired. I curled up in a ball right next to Dorothy's side. It was good to feel her warmth along my back, just as I used to feel the closeness of my mother and my littermates when we'd sleep all huddled together.

"Look! He's doing it!" Mona whispered, delighted.

I yawned again and closed my eyes. Time for a nap. It was nice to nap with a friend.

"Oh, good boy, Toby," I heard Mona say.

I wagged once for being a good boy. And then I fell asleep.

After a while—I didn't really know how long—I felt myself slowly awakening. First, my ears were aware of Dorothy's steady, slow breathing. Then my nose picked up her scent and Mona's and Patsy's and Fran's nearby.

"See? He's doing really well," I heard Patsy say softly. "Dorothy was having trouble getting any rest. With Toby beside her, she just drifted right off."

"Hmmm," I heard Fran say.

"He's such a good dog," Mona said. I knew those words. My eyes opened to take in my three friends. I wagged.

"Good dog, Toby!" Mona said again. She pulled a bag of treats out of a pocket in her jeans—so *that's* where she'd been hiding them!—and poured several into her palm. She offered them to me, and her voice was warm and happy. "Such good Lie Still!" she praised me.

I loved to hear her voice like that, but I had no idea why she was bringing up Lie Still again. I was happy to have the treats, though. After I'd gobbled them up, I stood on the bed and stretched.

"Careful, Toby." Mona picked me up cautiously. "Don't wake Dorothy."

She put me on the ground, and I shook all over. I felt good after my long run and my nap. It was probably time to go and look for Eddie. He might have some bacon.

I dodged between Fran's feet, and she let out a startled noise. Then I tore out of the room and dashed down the hall, dodging around some of my friends walking with their metal cages and one chair with wheels. "Oh, Toby!" I heard Mona groan, and she played Chase with me all the way to the kitchen.

12

A few days later, Mona and I were Training on the lawn—*again!*—when Patsy came out to visit us. "Fran wants to see us both," Patsy said to Mona.

"About Toby?" Mona asked. I could feel her anxiety spike, so I licked her hands.

"What else?" Patsy said with a sigh.

I followed Mona and Patsy into Fran's office. Fran was sitting behind her desk, and there was something new in a corner. It was big and reminded me a little of the metal cages some of my friends leaned on when they walked. I went over to sniff it. It did not smell fun.

Patsy settled down on the little couch, but Mona was too nervous to sit. I tugged at her shoelace.

"What's that?" Mona asked, eying the metal thing.

"A compromise," Fran said.

While Mona and Patsy looked at the metal thing, Fran went on.

"I know you've been training the dog more. Has it worked? Can he be a reliable therapy dog?"

Mona sighed. "He's getting better . . ."

"That's not what I asked."

"Well, no. Not yet," Mona admitted. "But everybody loves him, they really do!"

"He's been walking with people on the treadmill," Patsy said quietly. "They do more PT when he's there."

My ears perked. Were we going to do Treadmill?

"So I've seen." Fran nodded. "And I admit that he was helpful with Dorothy the other day. So here is my compromise. Toby can stay—"

"He can stay?" Mona burst out. Her face lit up with a smile. "Oh, thank you, Fran!"

I jumped up on my back legs to lick Mona's hand, wanting to join in her happiness. Besides, her fingers tasted like treats.

Fran held up a hand. "You didn't let me finish. He can stay, as long as he remains in the crate when he's not working. He can help the residents on the tread-mill, and he can play with the children who have rela-tives in the hospice wing. But other than that, he's got to be in the crate unless you're training him. We can't have him running through the halls anymore. That's final."

Mona's happiness drained away.

"In a crate?" she said. "But he's never had any crate training. He won't understand why he's being shut up. And he hasn't done anything wrong. He's just got a lot of energy."

"Nevertheless, that's my final decision," Fran said.

"Yes, ma'am," Patsy said.

I sat down and leaned against Mona's leg to make her feel better. Once all the people were done talking, she and I could have a good game of Chase. That would fix everything.

That night, after Mona fed me my dinner, we played in the TV room for a long time, wrestling with a rubber bone. It was excellent! Mona usually left right after giving me my food, but today she didn't seem to want to go.

"Mona," Patsy said, coming up to us with her purse over her shoulder. "Time to leave."

"Oh, Mom," Mona said sadly. She let go of the bone, and I seized it in my teeth and ran around the room in triumph. "I hate to shut him in there. He won't understand."

"I know. But he'll probably just sleep, honey. And you can let him out in the morning."

"If I'd just trained him better . . . I feel like such a failure, Mom."

"No, Mona. Sweetie, you're not a failure. Listen. We adopted Toby because the rancher told us he was very mellow and calm. That turned out to be a mistake. He was just tired because he was ill. And now he's better. That's not your fault or anybody's fault." Mona stood up, and Patsy hugged her. "You've been working so hard with him, but you're learning a lesson that's good for a trainer. You can't go against a dog's breed. You can't train a beagle not to run."

Mona sighed and hugged her mother back. Then she came to my side and pulled the chew toy from my teeth. I thought we were going to play more Tug—so exciting! But instead, Mona walked me down the hallway to the little room where my bed was kept.

To my surprise, the metal cage from Fran's office was in my room now. And my bed was inside it! So were the bowls with my food and water. Most bewildering of all, Mona tossed the rubber bone inside the open door of the cage. What an odd way to play!

Of course, I ran in to grab the toy. But when I turned back around so that Mona and I could wrestle some more, Mona shut the door of the cage in my face.

"Bye, Toby," she told me, and her voice quivered. "See you tomorrow!"

She departed very suddenly, leaving me behind.

People are very odd sometimes. But, well, food is food. I dropped the rubber bone, stuck my nose in my bowl, and began eating in big gulps. Soon I'd finished dinner and licked the bowl clean.

That was when I realized that I could not get out of the cage!

I pawed at the door and nudged it hard with my nose. It did not open.

I barked so that Mona would understand that she had made a mistake. Then she'd come back and get me.

But she didn't come back. No one did.

I tried getting my teeth around the wires. They tasted cold and bitter and horrible. And no matter how I chewed or tugged or twisted, I could not make them move an inch.

What had happened? Why was I shut in here? Who was going to come back and let me out?

If I truly belonged to Mona, she would not have left me in here. That was such an awful thought that I had to go back to my bed and lie down. But I couldn't sleep, so I began to chew and tug at the soft cloth that covered my bed, just like I used to chew on my feet when they itched and ached.

So Mona was not my person? Was that really true? Would someone else come and let me out of here? Eddie? Patsy? Tyler?

The cloth of my bed ripped, and something white and fuzzy popped out. It did not taste good at all, but I still nipped at it. Then I trapped it under one paw and pulled at it with my teeth until it came apart in shreds.

I don't know why I did these things, but they made me feel a little better.

After some time had passed and my bed couldn't be chewed anymore, I got up and bit the cage again. But it only hurt my teeth and my mouth.

And still, nobody came.

This was dreadful! I had never felt so alone, so abandoned, so lost. I could not stand it.

Somehow, I knew just what to do with feelings like this. I sat down, lifted up my muzzle, and let the sadness out in a long, mournful sound. "Arooooo! Aroooo!" I howled.

I did it over and over again.

Then, finally, *finally*, the door to my small room opened. Light from the hallway spilled in. There, in her wheelchair, was Dorothy! Grandad was pushing her, leaning on the handles of her chair.

"Toby!" Dorothy said.

I stopped howling. My tail even stirred to life. My friends had come! Thank goodness!

"Good thing I've been spending all that time on the treadmill with Toby!" Grandad said, wheeling Dorothy's

chair farther into the room. "I don't think I could have pushed this contraption otherwise. There! Can you get Toby's cage open?"

A couple of other friends were standing in the door, looking in, as Grandad moved Dorothy closer to me. She reached down and opened the lock on the door.

In a flash, I had shoved the door open and barreled through. I was out! I was free! I put my front feet in Dorothy's lap and licked her gentle hands. I raced around Grandad and licked his knees. I greeted all my friends in the hallway and then ran and ran, skidding around corners, sliding into a wall, jumping up and running some more.

Maybe I belonged to Grandad and Dorothy. Or maybe I didn't. I still wasn't sure. They'd come for me, though, and that was all that mattered. I was free, and I could have fun with all my friends, and I would never go back inside that cage again.

Never!

13

That night, I slept at the foot of Grandad's bed. The next morning, Mona came to feed me and let me outside. After that, she and Patsy and Grandad and Dorothy did a lot of talking. Then Mona and Patsy went into Patsy's office and talked some more.

I'd forgiven Mona for her mistake, shutting me up in that cage, so I went with them. But I got bored. When Fran came to the office door, I ran to greet her. She had never played with me yet, but there's always a first time. I wagged my tail and panted up at her face, trying to let her know that we'd had a lot of fun last night and could have some more now, if she'd join in.

But she ignored me. "Do you know what happened last night?" she demanded. "People got out of their rooms to play with the dog! The night staff went crazy trying to get everyone back to sleep!"

"Yes, I've heard," Patsy said.

"Toby's not used to the crate. He didn't understand," Mona said. She sounded worried.

Fran let out her breath in an exasperated sigh. "All right. The crate is not a success. Then the dog has to go outside at night. It's summer; he'll be fine. Dogs sleep outside all the time."

"I don't know," Mona said with a little worry still in her voice. "He's used to wandering around inside at night."

"That," said Fran sharply, "is one of the problems we are trying to fix."

I'd had enough of listening to people make words at each other, so I went off to look for someone to throw the ball for me.

That afternoon, after dinner, Mona took me outside. To my surprise, there was a new bed lying in the grass! My water bowl was next to it. I sniffed both. How strange.

"Your bed's going to be out here now, Toby," Mona said, rubbing behind my ears. "At least for a while. You just have to learn to be calm. No more howling at night, all right?"

I licked her hands and looked up at her. Was it time to go inside now?

Then she pulled a ball from her pocket. Perfect! My whole body leaped to attention. She threw the ball, and I bounded after it.

When I brought it back, Mona had gone!

Gone! How could she have forgotten how to play this game? I was supposed to get the ball, while she stood and waited until I brought it back to her. That's what she had always done before. What on earth had happened this time?

With the ball still in my mouth, I ran over to the door and waited in front of it. I had noticed that whenever I sat near a door, it opened. Usually, one of my friends would be standing beside it to say, "Hi, Toby. Come on in." Or "Okay, Toby. Out you go."

But this time, the door did not work, for some reason. It did not open. I was stuck on one side with my ball, and Mona was on the other!

I dropped the ball and barked so people would come and fix the door.

But no one came.

I whined. I scratched at the door. I put my front paws on it and barked some more.

Still no one came.

How could this be happening? All the old, lonely

feelings from last night came back in a rush, even stronger this time. I didn't even have the energy to howl, to let the world know that a lost, lonely, miserable dog was outside by himself.

I crept back to my new bed. It smelled very strange and new, not at all like a bed should smell, of dust and dirt and dog.

I curled up on the cushion with my nose on my tail. I wished my mother were here to wrap her body around mine and comfort me with her touch.

But no one was here. I was all alone.

It now felt like I didn't belong to anyone at all.

After a while, I fell asleep. There was nothing else to do. In the morning, light woke me, along with a squirrel sitting on a branch overhead and scolding me for being there.

I got up and shook and stretched. At least one good thing had come of my being left out here, all by myself—I didn't have to wait for anyone to let me out so I could pee.

Then something terrific happened.

The door opened! It worked again! And Mona was standing there, smiling at me!

I dashed inside and threw myself at her, trying to cuddle with her and lick her and run with her all at once, trying to tell her that something awful had happened, that I'd been left alone *all night long*, but that it was all right now because she'd come back at last. But she should never do that to me again!

"Okay, Toby. Okay, sweetie," she said over and over, stroking her hands all over me, from my head to my tail. "Come on now. Time for breakfast."

I knew that word. Breakfast! I began to feel better.

After breakfast, I did quick visits with all my friends. Eddie had not forgotten about bacon. Dorothy threw the ball for me. Grandad was sitting in a chair in his room, writing on a piece of paper with a pen. When I ran in, he looked up and laughed. He had a treat for me, which I was happy to accept.

"Quieter night this time, huh, Toby?" he asked, scratching my neck. I wagged for my name.

"How did Toby do outside all night?" another voice asked, and Tyler was standing in the doorway.

Another friend! I ran over to him to get more attention, and he and Grandad talked while I sniffed Tyler's shoes and pulled at his shoelaces until they were long and loose.

"I'm sorry I can't be there for your first meet," Grandad said to Tyler. "I wanted to cheer you on, but . . ."

"I know," Tyler said quietly as he retied his shoelaces. "I'll tell you all about it. Or you know Mom will video every minute. Hey, Toby, let's go find Mona. I have to ask her something."

I heard Mona's name and charged down the hallway to find her.

Once we found her in the TV room, Mona and Tyler stood and talked and talked and *talked*. I hunted around until I discovered one of my chew toys under a chair. I brought it over to them happily. Now they'd have something more interesting to do.

But they didn't understand. Humans often don't. Mona and Tyler just stood and talked and smiled at each other. I had to lie down and chew on the toy all by myself.

"You're not going to run with the team anymore?" Mona asked.

"Well, it's not really a team. Just sort of a summer club. They do have meets, though. And they said I could tag along, but the thing is, they've all been running since sixth grade, and they're a little older than me, too. A couple of them are going into high school in the fall. I can't really keep up, and it's kind of . . ."

"Yeah, I know, that doesn't sound too fun." Mona laughed, for not much reason that I could see.

"So I want to run by myself for a little while, until I'm better. Toby's good company, though. I like running with him. You think it's okay if he goes running with just me? I guess it's a little different from running with the whole club."

"Sure, I guess. Well, maybe we should ask Fran."

"Fran? The one who's in charge? She's kind of scary."

Mona laughed again. "I know! But she'll say yes, I'm sure, because she loves getting Toby out of here."

I perked up my ears for my name, but clearly, neither of them was about to pet me or play with me or give me a treat.

"She's crazy. My Grandad loves Toby. Everybody does!"

"I know. But we'll ask her about the running thing, anyway. Mom says she likes to be asked. I know—we'll get Mom to come with us. Fran will listen to Mom."

Tyler and Mona and Patsy went to talk to Fran. So much talking! Even Training was better than this.

Then Tyler left. "See you tomorrow morning, then, Toby," he said.

"A nice boy," Fran said to Patsy. "It was very responsible of him to come and check about running with Toby by himself."

I was bored with my chew toy by now, so I decided to lick Mona's ankles instead.

"I can certainly see that Mona thinks he's a nice boy," Fran said, and Mona picked me up and hugged me and put her face in my fur as if she didn't want anybody to see it.

It was very odd, but that night, Mona made the same mistake *again*! She put me in the backyard, threw a ball for me to chase, and forgot to wait for me to give it back to her!

How could I get her to understand? I barked and whined and scratched at the door and even let my sadness out with more of those long *aroooooo* howls. But Mona must not have been able to hear me, because she did not come back to get me until the sky had gotten light again in the morning.

Tyler came, too, that morning and took me outside so that we could run. But to my surprise, there were no other boys waiting for us outside the front door. Just Tyler.

I looked up at him, wondering where the boys had gone. Did we need to chase them?

But it seemed that we didn't, because Tyler just tightened up his shoelaces and started jogging down the road. I ran after him with a bark of delight, my lonely night in the yard forgotten.

If Tyler and I ran together, just him and me, did that mean I belonged to Tyler? It was a nice thought. But what about Mona? Even though she kept forgetting to bring me in from the yard, I still loved her. And I loved Eddie, too. And his bacon, of course.

It was very confusing, but I spotted a rabbit to chase, so I decided that was more important.

We ran a long time that morning, and when we got back, I was panting as hard as I could, with my tongue hanging out. Tyler found Mona to give her my leash, and I could tell she was glad to see me.

"Good, I'm glad you're back with Toby," she said to him. "We need him."

She let me drink most of my water bowl, which I was happy to do, and then she took me to the part of my home that I thought of as the Quiet Place.

We had not been there since the last time Mona and I had played Chase with Eddie. I looked up at Mona in surprise. Were we going to play Chase some more? I was pretty tired from my run. I didn't actually feel like Chase right now.

But it seemed that we weren't, because Mona took me to a room with a bed. Patsy was there, waiting for us.

A man was lying on the bed. I recognized him, even though I didn't know his name. He was one of my friends, and he kept treats in a jar by his bed for when I stopped by.

He didn't offer me a treat now, though. He just lay very still. And he smelled . . . different.

I lifted my nose in puzzlement. It was a strange odor, one I had not met before. He smelled tired. And quiet. And somehow, he smelled far away.

It made me feel confused and a little uneasy. I looked up at Mona in puzzlement and even let out a small whine.

"Now?" she asked Patsy. Her voice was hushed.

Patsy nodded. "Now."

Mona bent down and lifted me up to the bed next to the man. The sheets felt cool and soft against my feet, which were a little sore from my long run.

My friend did not seem to notice me. I sniffed at his face.

"Lie still," Mona said softly. "Toby, lie still."

That again? Whatever. I was too tired to play Training right now. I curled up against my friend with a sigh.

Time for a nap.

As I drifted off to sleep, I heard Mona and Patsy exchange a few words. Then a different voice joined in. It was quiet, but it was still fierce.

"What is the dog doing here? Get him out of the hospice wing!"

I felt my friend on the bed move very slightly. Slowly, he lifted one hand. He ran it down my back, his touch so light I could barely feel it.

He put his hand down on the sheet again. I opened my eyes and closed them again with a long sigh.

"Watch," I heard Patsy say to Fran. "He's giving comfort. Can't you see Martin relax with Toby there beside him? He doesn't have any family to be with him now. Just us and Toby. We can't take that away from him."

There was a long pause.

"Okay," Fran said at last. "But you've both got to stay here at all times. If there's any trouble, the dog has to leave at once."

"Of course," Patsy said. Her voice sounded as if she were smiling.

"Good boy, Toby," Mona told me. "Good Lie Still. Good boy."

I was glad that she thought I was a good boy, but all I wanted to do right now was sleep.

14

That was the last time I saw that particular friend. When I woke up, I was back in my own bed. It was funny. I got up and shook and trotted through the halls, sniffing, to see if I could smell him anywhere. But I could not. He was gone.

It was confusing, but there were still a lot of people to greet me and pet me and call me a good boy as I wandered around my home. This didn't mean, though, that everything was normal, because I still slept out in the yard! And the next day, Tyler came to get me in the morning for another run.

Running was the best!

Today, there was a squirrel to chase up a tree, and two trash cans to sniff, and several new friends to greet.

"Cute dog," they'd say. "Can I pet him?" "Can my kid say hi?" We'd stop so I could sniff new hands and lick new faces, and then we were off again, moving fast, with the wind in my nose and the freshness of new smells greeting me with every step.

That day, we did something even more exciting than usual. After jogging along a paved street for a while, Tyler turned a corner and we were on a dirt road. Dirt! I loved running on dirt. It felt softer to my paws, and it smelled so much better than that hard black surface that cars roll on.

And then Tyler took off my leash. Fantastic! I could race ahead and come back to him or dash off to investigate clumps of grass or chase grasshoppers or grab sticks. This was the best run we had ever been on.

Crows flew overhead, and I barked to let them know that we were running, and they could come with us if they liked. But they didn't pay attention.

There were giant dogs in the fields next to the road, with black-and-white splotches all over their bodies. Mostly they ignored us, but I barked at them, too, just because.

A warm breeze rushed past us, lifting my ears a little, ruffling my fur. My ears perked up. I lifted my nose high and sniffed with all my might.

That breeze had brought a familiar scent with it.

Tyler was a few feet behind me, and he was starting

to breathe in big gasps. "Okay, Toby," he wheezed. He stopped running and stood with his hands on his knees. "Toby? Time to head home."

I heard him say my name, but I didn't turn back to him. That scent! It had been a long time since I'd smelled it. It was telling me of something just up ahead.

"Toby!" Tyler called, but he didn't say "Come," so I knew we weren't doing Training. We were just running. And so I ran.

"Toby! No! Where are you going?" Tyler yelled, but I was far ahead of him now.

The smell grew stronger with every step. I recognized it! It was chickens and the big dogs who let people ride on their backs. It was dirt and grass and growing things. It was my first home! The Ranch!

And I was there!

Tyler was far enough back on the road that he could not stop me from wiggling under the rail of a fence and running across a lawn. A man was pushing a noisy machine across the grass, but I didn't stop to greet him.

The best scent of all was in my nose. Sadie! My mother!

There she was! Lying in the sun beside the house, with a braided rope in her mouth. Her head jerked up as I came tearing through the grass, and she jumped to her feet.

I tumbled into her, my tail wagging so hard it nearly toppled me over. She sniffed me as eagerly as I sniffed her, and I was so happy I had to do something with my feelings.

I leaped on the rope, grabbed it between my teeth, and shook it hard. Sadie was as happy as I was. I could tell because she snatched the rope, too, and we had a great game of Tug until she pulled too hard and I rolled over and over in the grass.

"Well," said the man who had been pushing the machine. "Where did you come from, huh?"

He'd left the machine and was standing, watching us play. Now he held out a hand, and I trotted up to him, still wagging as hard as I could. I knew him! I knew his smell, and his hands, and the soft shirt he had on, with its scent of sweat and dirt and grass. Walt!

"Wow, I think you're one of mine," Walt said, petting me. "Glad to be home, huh? Let me see your collar." He tugged gently at the metal tags that hung from the collar around my neck. "Toby? Really? You're Toby?"

I licked him for saying my name, and for being Walt, and for being there while I was so happy to see my mother again. She came and licked him, too, and then someone else called my name.

"Toby! Toby! I'm sorry. He got away from me. Toby!"

Tyler climbed over the fence that I had crawled under and jogged up to us, breathing hard.

"This your dog?" Walt asked him.

"No, that's Toby," Tyler said, holding out his hand to me. When I trotted over to lick him too, to show that I was happy he had joined the reunion, he snapped my leash onto my collar. That didn't seem quite fair. How was I supposed to play with my mother now?

"He lives at the assisted living place," Tyler went on. "But I take him for a run sometimes."

"The assisted living place? That's six miles down the road!" Walt said. "You ran all that way? With Toby?"

Tyler nodded. Walt shook his head.

"I can hardly believe it. Once that little guy wouldn't run to save his life!" Tyler looked puzzled, and Walt chuckled. "Yeah, I guess you don't know it, but he was born here. That's Sadie, his mother. No wonder he came tearing in here like a rocket!"

"No kidding!" Tyler grinned and petted my mother, who greeted him happily and then came back to sniff me some more. "Toby, that's why you took off like that. I was worried I was going to lose you!"

"Well, he's a fine-looking dog now," Walt said. "I never would have thought he'd grow up like that. And he's still at that assisted living place? Working there?"

Tyler nodded.

"Good," Walt said. "He's got a purpose, then. All dogs need a purpose. They need a job to do. And he ran six miles!" He looked impressed. "You two want a ride back? I can take you in the truck."

Tyler shook his head. "No, thanks. We'll get back. I have to stick with it, or I'm not going to get better. And I have to get better. Soon."

Suddenly, he sounded sad. What a strange time to be sad! I licked his knees, which tasted sweaty and delicious. Then I licked my mother's nose and the toe of Walt's shoe.

"Well, good for you," Walt said. "But I'll get you something to drink before you go. And some water for Toby."

Walt gave me a delicious bowl of cool water. Fabulous! He handed Tyler something yellow and sweet-smelling in a glass, since people don't like to drink out of bowls. I don't know why.

Tyler guzzled down his drink almost as fast as I drank my water. Then he said good-bye to Walt and I said good-bye to my mother Sadie, and we started running again, slower than before but steadily, heading home.

I thought about Sadie, my mother, as I trotted by Tyler's side. Sadie belonged to Walt. She had stayed there with him even when my brothers and sisters and I had all left.

Now I was leaving again with Tyler. Maybe I

belonged to Tyler after all? But I still wasn't sure about that.

I hoped one day I would find out.

After that, Tyler and I ran together most days. I always got excited to see him in the mornings when he was wearing his white shoes that smelled of rubber and tar and dirt from the street and sweat from his feet. Such a delicious odor! I couldn't understand why he didn't wear those shoes all the time.

When I smelled those shoes on his feet, it usually meant that we were going to run to the Ranch! Sadie and I would sniff each other and play Chase and Wrestle and It's My Stick and You Can't Have It, and Tyler and Walt would watch us and laugh. Then Tyler would drink a glass of that sweet yellow stuff and we'd run back.

One day, to my surprise, we ran *past* the Ranch! I stopped and whined, reminding Tyler of the way we were supposed to go.

That day, Tyler had kept my leash on, and he pulled at me, insisting that we go *his* way. What were we doing?

"Wait and see, Toby," he told me, and we ran longer on the dirt road than we had ever done. Finally, we turned around, and *then* we went to the Ranch so that my mother and I could play.

At last!

When we returned to my home after these runs, I was always tired and ready for a big drink and a good nap. Tyler would hand my leash to Mona, and she'd usually take me to rest on a bed with one of my friends.

"Lie still," she'd say. "Lie still!"

Sometimes I wondered if she'd forgotten that my name was Toby and decided to call me Lie Still instead.

Tyler came to visit other times, too, not just in the morning for our runs. One afternoon, Mona saw him come in the front door. She had me on my leash, and she and I went up to greet him.

I sniffed his shoes, but they were not the admirably smelly ones he wore when we ran. I was still glad to see him, though, so I jumped up and put my paws on his knees to tell him so.

"Are you going to visit your grandfather?" Mona asked. "Could Toby practice Lie Still with him?"

"I'm sure he'd love that," Tyler said, scratching behind my ears. I knew the word *love,* but it was funny how sad Tyler's voice sounded when he said it. *Love* was not a sad word.

"Okay, come on, Toby," Mona said. "Come with us."

I knew Come, too, so I followed her down the hall to Grandad's room. I was glad to see him! So I leaped up on the bed and put my paws on the book he was reading so that I could lick his chin.

"No, Toby," Mona said. "Lie still!"

That again? I sat down and wagged my tail, looking at her hopefully to see if this would please her. She was standing next to Tyler. She sighed.

That morning, Tyler and I had been on a good long run, and I'd had a marvelous game of You Can't Catch Me with my mother. Whenever I saw Tyler, I thought about running to the Ranch. And that made me think of taking a nap.

I'd taken a nap next to Dorothy after our run this morning. When I woke up, Mona had told me, "Good dog, Toby. Good Lie Still."

Now, on Grandad's bed, I tilted my head to look at Mona in puzzlement. Was I a good dog for napping? Napping did not seem like my other tricks. It was not like Sit or Down or Shake. It was just . . . napping. Because I was sleepy.

But Mona said I was a good dog when I napped. Other times, I was not always a good dog. But every time I napped after a run, I was. Was that Lie Still?

I wasn't very sleepy now. But it seemed to make Mona so happy when I just lay there. Lie Still. Maybe, even though I wasn't tired, I'd pretend to take a nap. Maybe that would make Mona happy!

I curled up next to Grandad's side. The warmth of his body felt good next to mine. I even sighed, without thinking about it, just as I often did when I was ready for a nap.

"Oh, good boy, Toby," Mona said.

"Don't move, Grandad," Tyler said.

"Good, Toby. Good Lie Still!" Mona praised. She was happy! I was a good dog! I wagged the very tip of my tail, just so that she would know I'd heard her. I knew what Lie Still meant, now.

Mona came to the bed and stroked her hand along my back, telling me over and over that I was a good boy, that I was doing a good Lie Still. Tyler came and petted me, too, which was very nice. Two hands rubbing my back made me wiggle with delight. But then I remembered that Lie Still meant pretend napping, and I forced myself to be quiet again.

"Mona, you did it! He's got it!" Tyler was grinning. "You're a great dog trainer!"

He picked up his hand from my back. He reached to put it on my head again, but Mona's hand was already there.

Tyler left his hand on Mona's. They both stopped petting me until I picked up my head and looked at them with a bit of reproach in my eyes.

Wasn't I doing a good Lie Still? Wasn't this what they'd both wanted? Why had they stopped telling me what a good dog I was?

They remembered then and petted me some more. Sometimes people just need reminding.

15

A couple of weeks after my first Lie Still with Grandad, Mona came to get me. It was afternoon, and Dorothy and I were playing Chase the Ball outside in the yard.

"Sorry, Dorothy, but Toby's got a very important appointment!" Mona said, clipping my leash onto my collar.

She took me to a car. Patsy sat in the front seat and drove, while Mona and I sat in the back. I pressed my nose to the window, which was open just a crack at the top. Wind rushed in, packed full of smells that made me dizzy with excitement. So wonderful!

When the car stopped and we got out, I looked around in surprise to see all the people there. So many new friends! I wagged and wagged as Mona took me on my leash through the crowd, and people smiled and stopped to pet me. One little girl even gave me a crunchy, salty treat from a bag that rustled in her hand. I liked this place very much.

"Come on, Toby. The race is going to start soon," Mona urged, tugging on my leash.

She took me to where the crowd was thickest. A group of boys was standing together on the grass, and a thin dirt road, like the one Tyler and I followed to get to the Ranch, led off into some trees.

"Good. We're just in time," Mona said. "Here, Toby, do you want to see?"

She picked me up and held me. I squirmed so that I could lick her chin.

Someone shouted, and the boys lined up across the grass. Then I began to squirm harder in Mona's arms.

Tyler! Tyler was there with all the other boys! My whole body quivered with eagerness. This morning, Tyler had not come to get me for my run, but he was here! Now! Shouldn't I go to him?

A man was standing near the boys, and he put a hand up in the air. He was holding some kind of a toy in it, something black and shiny. The toy made a loud noise. I twitched in surprise. And all the boys started running toward the forest.

Running!

I squirmed harder and whined. Tyler was running without me! This wasn't what was supposed to happen. When Tyler ran, I belonged to him!

"Toby, take it easy!" Mona said. She put me down on the grass and fumbled with my leash.

I had to get to Tyler! I lunged forward. My leash slipped through Mona's fingers. "Toby!" she shouted, but I was too busy to take care of her right at that moment.

I tore across the grass, my leash trailing behind me, whipping like a snake. I dodged trampling feet and grabbing hands. The boys had nearly reached the trees by now. I'd catch them! After all the running Tyler and I had done, my legs were strong and the pads of my paws were tough. Those boys could not get away from me.

Now I was in the forest, and Tyler was right ahead of me. He was running behind the other boys, just as he used to. Pretty soon, I was at his heels.

"Toby?" Tyler gasped in surprise, looking down at me.

I yipped up at him happily. He'd forgotten to come and get me for this run, but I forgave him. Now that we were running together, everything was all right.

It was better than all right. It was perfect!

"Good . . . dog . . . Toby," Tyler said, pulling in big breaths between his words. He reached down and, without missing a step, unsnapped my leash, winding it around his fist.

I darted around Tyler's feet so that I could run ahead of him. Where was the Ranch? Weren't we going there? I was afraid Tyler might have gotten confused and taken the wrong road. I was sure I could find the right one.

No matter how hard I sniffed, I could not smell a whiff of Sadie or Walt on the warm breeze that drifted to me. But when we broke out from under the trees, our path ran alongside a fenced-in meadow. On the other side of the fence were some of those enormous black-and-white dogs. So obviously, we would get to the Ranch soon.

I sped up so I could bark at the big dogs. The big dogs ignored me. They usually did. I wondered why they never barked back.

Tyler sped up, too. He stayed close.

The pack of boys ahead of us had begun to spread out, some running a bit slower, some pushing ahead of the rest. A boy in dark shorts was running just in front of us as we jogged along the fence that held the big dogs in. I passed him, and then another boy. Somewhere up ahead, the Ranch would be waiting, and I'd get a big bowl of cool water and play with Sadie and greet Walt. I could hardly wait.

I glanced back and discovered to my great joy that Tyler had finally figured out how to play Chase Me! He was right behind me. I wagged my tail for him and looked ahead again.

Slowly, we passed boy after boy. Our trail took us back under more trees and over a small bridge with a skinny creek trickling underneath. Tyler's feet pounded on the wooden boards, and my claws scratched them. I would have liked to stop for a drink, but I didn't want to lose this sensational game that we were all playing. A drink could come later.

A boy ahead of us tried to jump over a log that lay in the path. He stumbled, though, and fell to his hands and knees. I bounded over the log easily and stopped to check on the fallen boy. I licked his face. It was nice and sweaty. Tasty!

"You okay?" Tyler shouted from behind.

"Yeah . . . okay . . . ," the boy gasped, getting slowly to his feet. Tyler hurdled the log before the boy could start running again, and I dashed out in front of Tyler once more. Our path wound in slow curves and then led us down a slope. I could see a break in the trees ahead and sunlight shining on grass.

Only one boy was ahead of Tyler and me now, halfway down the slope. He wore a light-colored T-shirt and dark shoes. When he looked back over his shoulder, I barked at him happily. He knew how to play Chase Me, too! He was asking me to come and get him!

I was delighted to oblige.

I put on speed as we headed down the slope, and Tyler, breathing hard now, stayed close behind. We were going to catch that other boy! Any second now!

The boy in the dark shoes was right in front of us when we broke out from under the shadows of the trees and into the sunlight. But he was breathing hard, and his legs were starting to wobble a bit with each step.

I tore around the boy, my claws digging deep into the earth. Now I was running all by myself, ahead of Tyler and all of the pack. I looked back to be sure that they understood what to do. It was their turn to play Chase Me now!

The boy in the dark shoes was wobbling more and more. He began to slow down. Tyler did not. He ran steadily, not fast but never faltering. He drew close to the other boy. For a short time they ran side by side. Then Tyler slowly pulled ahead.

It was funny. Tyler used to like running behind all the other boys. Then he had wanted to run just with me. Now it seemed as if his favorite thing was to run with lots of boys again, but in front, not behind.

At least, the smile on his face as he passed the boy in the dark shoes made it look like being in front was his favorite thing. But then that smile faded.

I turned to look ahead and saw that a big hill was rising up in front of us. I charged up it, looking back often to encourage Tyler and the other boy to remember the rules of Chase Me. I was in the front now, and they had to catch me if they could.

Tyler was going slower now. The smile was off his face. But his feet were still steady on the ground. The boy in the dark shoes was behind him, and even from where I was running, I could hear how hard that boy was panting.

More boys were starting to jog out from the trees behind us. Great! We could all play together!

A sound drifted to my ears from over the top of the hill. People were shouting and cheering. They sounded excited and happy. They should come and run with us. They'd be even happier!

A warm breeze brought a scent to my nose. Mona! She was one of the people up ahead! I wanted to be with her, so I put on a little extra speed and reached the top of the hill.

I looked back to check on Tyler. He was still jogging after me. The boy in the dark shoes had stopped running and started walking. A few of the other boys were doing the same.

What a silly thing to do.

I looked ahead and saw that we'd run in a big circle

and come back to where we'd started. It wasn't nearly as far a run as the Ranch. Why hadn't we gone to the Ranch? Tyler must have gotten very lost. Oh well.

I could hear and see Mona now, as well as smell her. She was at the bottom of the hill, waving and shouting my name and Tyler's.

I ran to her, and she dropped to her knees to greet me. "Toby, you silly boy!" she kept saying. She grabbed hold of my collar.

Then Mona looked up. "Tyler! Tyler!" she shouted, jumping and waving.

Tyler was running down the hill now. His stride was wide, and his back was straight. I pulled on the collar so Mona would let me run to him. It was what I was supposed to do.

"No, Toby," she said, pulling back. I whined impatiently. She didn't understand. I looked up at her, trying to explain it with my eyes. Tyler was running. I was supposed to run with him.

"Oh well . . . ," Mona said and let go.

Wonderful! I raced after Tyler, barking at him happily, circled around his feet a few times, and jogged with him the rest of the way down the hill.

Tyler stopped running and put his hands on his knees and panted and panted. All the people clapped, and there was a lot of yelling. Breathless, he put my

leash back on. After a little while, the rest of the boys staggered over the hill and down to where we were waiting, and everybody clapped and yelled some more.

I wagged and wagged. All these people seemed very pleased. I must have been a very good dog.

After all the clapping and shouting and talking was over, Tyler drank a lot of water from a plastic bottle and poured some more over his head, and Mona poured some from another bottle into her hand for me to lap up. Then Mona pulled on my leash, and we went back to the place where all the cars were parked. One car pulled up and stopped for us to get in. Tyler and Mona sat together in the back seat with me.

Patsy was sitting in the front seat. Mona and Tyler were laughing, and both of them talked at the same time. They said my name a lot and Tyler's, too, and Patsy smiled, but she didn't seem as happy.

Then she said something back to them, and all their happiness went away, too. Just like that.

I was confused and looked from Tyler to Mona. Was something wrong? Had I been a bad dog? I sat in case that was what they wanted. I held up a paw for Tyler to shake.

He took it. "Good boy, Toby," he said, but his voice still sounded miserable.

I did Lie Still, curled up against Mona. She rubbed my ears. I was beginning to think I hadn't done anything wrong, but it was still hard to understand how all the happiness in that car could change to sadness so quickly.

"We'll go back now," Patsy said soberly, and she began to drive.

When we got back home, I jumped out of the car. Fran was waiting for us at the doorway.

"Your mom's already in the hospice wing with your grandfather," she said to Tyler. "We'll go right there." She looked down at me. "The dog's a mess. Mona, take him and get him cleaned up."

Tyler bent down and picked me up. He held me and put his face in my fur, and I felt his body relax just a little.

"It's just a little mud," Patsy said gently. "I don't think it matters all that much."

Fran looked at Tyler and at me. And for the first time, I did not feel like a bad dog around her.

"Yes, of course," she said gently. "You're right." She reached out a hand and stroked my back. "Good dog, Toby."

16

Tyler put me down on the floor, and we went along the hallway in a pack—Patsy, Fran, Mona, Tyler, and me. Mona kept hold of my leash. In a moment, I saw that we were headed for the Quiet Place.

"I don't think you've been to this wing before," Fran said to Tyler as we walked. "It's just a place where we can take very good care of people like your grandfather. Everything is about keeping them comfortable, about taking care of them and their families. Whatever your grandfather needs, we'll make sure that he has it. And I've been in touch with your mother. She and your father will be here as soon as they can."

Tyler nodded. I looked up into his face and Mona's,

trying to decide why everyone was so sad. We'd had so much fun running. What had happened?

Fran opened a door, and Tyler went inside. He reached out for Mona's hand, the one holding my leash, and held it. So Mona and I went inside with him. Patsy and Fran stayed in the doorway, looking in.

Grandad was there! He was sitting up in a bed, leaning back against the headboard. I ran up to the bed, wagging hard, and put my muddy front paws up on the quilt, trying to tell him what a good time we'd had, Tyler and I, running along the track. How we hadn't found the Ranch and Sadie and Walt, but it was all right, because we'd played Chase Me with lots of boys.

Grandad moved his hand, more slowly than he usually did, to rub my ears.

"How'd you do?" he asked Tyler. His words came more slowly, too.

"I won," Tyler said, a little shakily. "Toby and I won. He ran the whole thing with me, Grandad."

Grandad grinned. "Of course he did. And what about this young lady? Is she your girlfriend yet?"

Tyler groaned. "Grandad!"

Mona spoke up almost at the same time Tyler did. "Yes," she said.

Grandad chuckled. "I thought so."

"Grandad? What happened?" Tyler asked. I dropped

my feet down to the floor so I could look up at him better. "Are you sick?"

"It's the old ticker, I'm afraid." Grandad had to stop talking to draw in a breath. "Just ran out of time. Sit here with me awhile, will you?"

Tyler sat down in a chair. Mona sat next to him and held on to his hand. There was so much sadness in that room that I sat down on Tyler's feet and whined. I wished we could go outside and run and run so fast that we'd leave all of this sorrow behind.

For the next day or two, Tyler and I still went for a run in the mornings. But after that, we'd go right to Grandad's room. Mona came, too, and a woman Tyler called "Mom" and a man he called "Dad" were there a lot as well. Sometimes Grandad talked to us and had the energy to reach up and scratch my ears. Sometimes he just lay still.

A few days after Tyler and I had run in the woods with all the other boys, Patsy came to find me. I was outside on the lawn, bringing the ball back to Dorothy.

"I'm afraid I need Toby, Dorothy," Patsy said.

"I'm sorry to hear that," Dorothy said quietly. I laid the ball in her lap and ran over to Patsy, who gave me a treat.

"Come, Toby. I have a job for you," she said, and she

walked with me down the hall to the Quiet Place. I was not surprised when we headed for Grandad's new room.

Tyler was there, and Mona, too. Mom was sitting in a chair near Grandad's bed, and Dad was leaning over her with an arm around her shoulders.

Grandad was asleep, leaning back on his pillows. His breathing sounded like Tyler's after he and I had finished our morning runs.

I wanted to say hello to Grandad, so I jumped up on the bed. He didn't move. I sniffed at his face. There was a smell I recognized, a faint one that somehow told me Grandad was far away, too far to rub my ears or feed me a treat or call me by my name.

I knew what to do. I did Lie Still.

"Good boy, Toby," Patsy said softly. "Shall I leave you together?"

"Yes, thank you," Dad said. His voice was hoarse.

Tyler came over to the bed and stroked my head. He ran a hand along my back. "Good-bye, Grandad. I love you," he said softly.

Mom and Dad came close to the bed, too. Mona hesitated, but Tyler held out his hand to her, and she reached over to take it.

I did Lie Still, feeling the warmth of Grandad's side along my back. All these people were here with Grandad because they loved him. I could feel the love coming from them and how it wrapped around Grandad and held him close.

Grandad belonged to all these people.

And I did, too.

It was a new thought for me, and it made me so happy my tail wanted to wag, but I didn't let it. I knew tail wagging was not part of Lie Still.

My life was going to be different from my mother's. She belonged to one person, to Walt. But I did not. I wasn't Mona's dog, or Patsy's, or Tyler's, or Eddie's. I belonged to all my friends. I was everyone's dog.

I was surrounded by people who loved me, just like Grandad was.

Suddenly, I understood that I was the luckiest dog in the world.

STARSCAPE BOOKS
Reading & Activity Guide to
Toby's Story:
A Dog's Purpose
Puppy Tale
By W. Bruce Cameron
Ages 8–12; Grades 3–7

Synopsis

In W. Bruce Cameron's *Toby's Story: A Dog's Purpose Puppy Tale,* beagle puppy Toby teaches his newfound human friends that you *can* teach a new dog new tricks, but it takes a lot of patience and work. The people who train and treasure him teach Toby some vital life lessons, too. Fun-loving but sensitive Toby narrates the story. Toby describes his cozy early puppyhood on the Ranch with his mom and littermates; being adopted by nursing-home therapist Patsy and her animal-loving daughter, Mona; his battle with an energy-sapping undiagnosed allergy; and, most important, his development into a successful therapy dog, beloved by the residents and staff of the nursing home, where Patsy works (though Patsy's boss Fran is tough to win over)! Through poignant and sometimes puzzling interactions with a variety of people, young and old, happy and sad, healthy and sick, Toby discovers his true home, his "pack," and his purpose.

Reading *Toby's Story: A Dog's Purpose Puppy Tale* with Your Children

Pre-Reading Discussion Questions

1. In *Toby's Story: A Dog's Purpose Puppy Tale*, Toby, a beagle puppy, is the main character and narrator. Have you read other stories, or seen movies, with dog or animal protagonists? Was the animal itself the narrator or did a person tell the story? Do you prefer that it be one or the other? How or why does it make the story more, or less, interesting to you as a reader (or viewer)?

2. From your own experience, or from observing someone else's special connection with a dog, what are your ideas about what a dog's (or other pet's) purpose, or purposes, might be?

3. Do you think it is important to feel like you have a special purpose, or role, in your family, school, or community? Why?

Post-Reading Discussion Questions

1. As the narrator, beagle puppy Toby describes things from a candid, canine perspective. For example, in Chapter 1, commenting on horses he sees beyond his enclosure, Toby says: "Far away was another pen with very big, long-legged dogs inside it. One of them ac-

tually had a person riding on its back. Amazing!" Can you think of other examples from the text where Toby shares a funny impression, or *mis*impression, of someone or something? Can you cite some examples of wise, or thoughtful, observations Toby makes about human nature or life, from his unique, "dog's-eye" point of view?

2. In Chapter 2, Toby's feet become painful and itchy. How does this issue with his paws affect Toby's behavior? How does it affect his owner (Walt's) and visitors' impressions of Toby? How is he different than a typical beagle?

3. When his sister Tabitha gets adopted, Toby comments: "It was a little sad, but it was right, too. Dogs belonged with human families. Human families needed dogs." Do you agree with Toby? Do you have, or wish you had, a dog? How does (or could) having a dog make a difference in your family?

4. In Chapter 3, why is Mona's mom (Patsy) reluctant to adopt Toby, when she learns that he is a beagle? Once they decide to bring Toby to live at the nursing home where Patsy works, Mona explains Toby's role of therapy dog, telling him: "People can give the patients their medicine and help them get into wheelchairs and stuff like that. But they can't really make them happy. That's what you can do. You can make people happy." Do you agree with Mona that a puppy can help elderly residents in a nursing home in ways

that a human can't? Explain why you agree or disagree.

5. Toby loves that he and Mona spend time with lots of new friends, like Trent and his Grandad. But Toby wonders, in Chapter 4, who his actual owner is since he interacts with so many people each day, and he is left alone at night: "Which one did I belong to? Who was my new human family?" Why do you think it is so important to Toby to figure out who he belongs to, or who "belongs" to him?

6. When the vet diagnoses Toby's gluten allergy, Mona and Patsy feel guilty for not realizing the problem sooner, but Toby "forgives" them and is just glad he has more energy to run and play. How does Toby "meet" Eddie, who runs the kitchen at the nursing home?

7. In Chapter 6, Patsy's boss Fran asks: "What happened to our calm little puppy?" Can you explain how solving Toby's allergy problem leads to a different problem? How is doing Training with Mona going to help this problem? What does Toby think of Training?

8. In Chapter 7, Toby struggles when Patsy and Mona try to teach him the Lie Still command, but he has a successful encounter, too. How does Toby help his new friend Dorothy, another resident at the nursing home?

9. How does Toby's curiosity lead him to encounter Trent and his running group? What does Toby observe about Trent when he (Trent) is running with

the other boys? What advice does Grandad offer when Trent admits running isn't going too well?

10. How does Toby add happiness to a very sad day for the family who visits the nursing home in Chapter 10? What does Toby notice about Fran when she is with that family?

11. The nursing home residents love Toby, and some residents (including Grandad) even exercise more because Toby does Treadmill with them, but Fran still has doubts about Toby. What "compromise" does Fran introduce in Chapter 12? How does this lead to some late-night chaos at the nursing home, including Grandad and Dorothy teaming up to "free" Toby?

12. After the nighttime incident, Fran insists that Toby sleep outside, but he continues to play an important daytime role at the nursing home. How does Toby help Martin in the "Quiet Place," for example?

13. How does being Trent's running buddy (when Trent decides to practice separately from his running club for a bit) lead Toby back to his "first home", the Ranch? When Trent follows Toby to the Ranch, he meets Toby's former owner Walt. Why is Walt happy to learn from Trent that Toby is "working" at the nursing home?

14. What does Toby finally understand about Lie Still in Chapter 14? Why is it so important for him to know this particular "trick" for his role at the nursing home?

15. In Chapter 15, Trent wins his first cross-country race. How is Toby (unexpectedly) able to support Trent in this event? What sad circumstances over-shadow Trent's victory?

16. In the final chapter, how does Grandad's situation help Toby finally understand who they *both* (Grandad and Toby) "belong" to? Did reading this story change how you think about how pets and people love and "belong" to each other?

Post-Reading Activities

Take the story from the page to the pavement with these fun and inspiring activities for the dog lovers in your family.

1. CHANGE YOUR *FURSPECTIVE*!

Invite your child/children, and interested friends or family members to follow author W. Bruce Cameron's lead, and visualize the world from a dog (or other pet's) point of view. Gather markers, crayons, colored pencils, or paints, and white paper or poster board. Each of you can choose a dog or pet, which belongs to your family, or to another friend or relative, and draw or paint a scene (such as, a home/habitat; going for a walk; feeding time; or another pet-person interaction) from that animal's point of view, keeping in mind the animal's size, mobility, environment, and how keen or limited its senses are. Compare completed pictures, discussing how each of you envisioned your chosen animal's view of the world. (If several people drew the same pet, you can consider similarities and differences in the final pictures.) As "artists," discuss if it was easy or hard to look at the world, and try to represent it, from a different perspective!

2. **FOLLOW MY BREED**

Each breed has specific characteristics, which can make dogs of that breed more, or less, suited for different families, "jobs," or purposes. Beagles like Toby, for example, often are used as hunting dogs, and usually have a lot of energy, and love to run and chase. Toby was friendly and liked to meet new people, but if circumstances had been different—for example, if Toby hadn't had the allergy, which initially made him seem more mellow and less active than a typical dog of his breed—Patsy and Mona might not have selected Toby, or a beagle, to be a therapy dog at the nursing home. Together with your child, research dog breeds at the library or online. (HINT: Check out the American Kennel Club's website, http://www .akc.org). Choose 5–10 breeds. Using construction paper, poster board, stickers, markers, stencils, images cut from magazines or printed (if permissible) from breeders' or other dog-friendly websites, design and make a poster or brochure, which provides helpful information and fun images of each breed. You can even bring your finished poster or brochure to a local animal shelter, or rescue organization, and offer it as a resource to help potential pet owners make informed choices, which will benefit the people *and* pets involved.

3. **HOW CAN YOU HELP?**

Just like Mona and Toby worked as a team (with help from Mona's mom Patsy) at the nursing home, you and your child(ren) can participate in, or promote, the work of therapy dogs, and help people who might benefit from canine companionship. If you and your child want to learn about training your family dog, if you have one, to become a therapy dog (with you working as the dog's handlers), The Alliance of Therapy Dogs (ATD's) website (http://www.therapydogs.com) is a good resource for information about certification programs, testing, training, and opportunities for therapy dog/handler teams. Or, if you have a well-mannered family dog, you might consider bringing your child, together with the pup, to visit relatives or friends, who don't have a pet of their own, but might appreciate some of your dog's love and attention. Maybe your dog can leave his or her loving paw prints on people's hearts, just like Toby does! If you don't have a family dog, you and your child can still learn about, and support, the important work of therapy dogs. Brainstorm a list of friends or relatives whose dogs might be great candidates for therapy dogs. Perhaps you can invite those folks to an information session, which you and your child host. Kids can make posters and flyers for the event, to help inform and inspire guests to get involved.

Reading *Toby's Story*: *A Dog's Purpose Puppy Tale* in Your Classroom

These Common Core-aligned writing activities may be used in conjunction with the pre- and post-reading discussion questions above.

1. **Point of View**
   Toby's Story: *A Dog's Purpose Puppy Tale* is told from perceptive pup Toby's point of view. With a big heart and "beagle eye," Toby shares his curious, humorous, hopeful vision of the world. Ask students to think about a family or classroom pet, or an animal they've seen outside in nature or at a zoo. Invite them to write 2–3 paragraphs describing a typical day from that creature's perspective. As author W. Bruce Cameron does so skillfully and thoughtfully with Toby, encourage students to try to imagine what the world looks, sounds, smells, tastes, and feels like from their chosen animal's point of view. What do people and their activities look like from the animal's perspective? Does the animal have interactions with humans, or other animals, and what are those like? How and where

does the animal eat, sleep, exercise, or socialize? How does this animal view its place, or purpose, in the larger world?

2. **Born to Run**

    In a one-page essay, explore the central role running plays in the plot and theme of *Toby's Story: A Dog's Purpose Puppy Tale,* and in the lives of the book's key characters (human and canine). Invite students to discuss the different emotions, memories, worries, joys, or challenges that running brings up for each of these characters. Consider, for example, what readers learn in Chapter 4 about Trent and Grandad's connections to running. What does running mean to them individually, and how is running a part of Trent and Grandad's relationship with each other? How does Toby feel about running? How did Toby's reluctance to run and be active (when his paws started troubling him) affect his early life? How does having his allergy diagnosed and rediscovering the pleasures of running impact (both positively and negatively) Toby's role and relationships at the nursing home? Encourage students to use relevant examples, quotes, and details from the text, as well as making inferences from characters' running-related dialogue, actions, or interactions.

3. **Text Type: Opinion Piece**

    In *Toby's Story: A Dog's Purpose Puppy Tale,* Patsy and Mona hope Toby will be a therapy dog that can bring happiness and comfort to the elderly, sick, and sometimes dying, residents at the nursing home where Patsy works. Patsy and Mona give far more weight to the smiles and joy Toby inspires every day (and night) at the nursing home, than to his difficulty mastering certain skills, hallway runs, occasional "puddles," or rogue howling. Fran (the head of the nursing home), on the other hand, is concerned about the potential risks Toby—as an (increasingly) energetic puppy—poses to safety, cleanliness, and routine. She worries that Toby might trip residents, or be disruptive, especially in the hospice wing, where people need peace. Invite your students to share *their* opinion on whether there are more pros or cons to having Toby as a therapy dog at the nursing home. Ask students to state and support their opinion in a one-page essay, being sure to include details and "evidence" from the story to defend their position.

4. **Text Type: Narrative**

    Toby's Story: A Dog's Purpose Puppy Tale is told entirely from Toby's perspective. As the narrator, Toby can "explain" his actions and reactions directly to the reader, who only learns what Toby knows, observes, or experiences. Invite students to explore how the story might be different if they picked another character (such as Mona, Patsy, Fran, Trent, Grandad, or Dorothy) to be the narrator. Ask students to write 1–3 pages in the voice of that character, describing a scenario involving Toby (such as the day Toby arrives at the nursing home; the night he howls in the crate; an outdoor or treadmill run; or another joyful, or sorrowful, situation). Using, or expanding on, details from the text, have the "new narrator" comment on how Toby's presence affects their time visiting, living, or working at the nursing home.

5. **Research & Present: OF HOUND MIND AND BODY: MEET THE BEAGLE**

Since the main character of *Toby's Story: A Dog's Purpose Puppy Tale* is a beagle, readers learn about beagles as they get to know Toby, and follow him from newborn pup to therapy dog. Invite students to do online and library research to learn more about the happy hound dog. (HINT: Check out The National Beagle Club of America's website at http://www .nationalbeagleclub.org.) Students can explore the beagle's history, health, temperament, physicality, popularity as a pet, and even as an icon—think of cartoonist Charles Schulz's *Snoopy* character! Students can share all the data they "dig up," in a PowerPoint or other multi-media style presentation.

6. **Research & Present: READY, PET, GO! ANIMALS HELPING PEOPLE**

In *Toby's Story: A Dog's Purpose Puppy Tale,* readers learn about therapy dogs from Toby's experience, but dogs and other animals can help people in a variety of ways. In addition to therapy dogs, there are service dogs and emotional support animals (or ESAs). The benefits and applications of Animal-assisted Therapy (AAT) continue to be explored in a wide variety of settings, from schools to rehabilitation centers. Have students work in pairs or small groups, to research a topic or question they choose, related to therapy or service dogs, or emotional support animals. (HINT: Check out The Alliance of Therapy Dogs (therapydogs .com) or The International Association of Human-Animal Interaction Organizations http://www.iahaio .org.) Have students organize and present their research findings in an oral presentation, supported by colorful visual and written aids.

Supports English Language Arts Common Core Writing Standards: W.3.1, 3.2, 3.3, 3.7; W.4.1, 4.2, 4.3, 4.7; W.5.1, 5.2, 5.3, 5.7; W.6.2, 6.3, 6.7; W.7.2, 7.3, 7.7